CHANGING DREAMS

BEAR LAKE DREAMERS

KIRSTEN OSBOURNE

UNLIMITED DREAMS

INTRODUCTION

Alyssa Romriell feels her life spiraling out of control. Her career is going well, but her love interest is becoming less and less interested in her. She knows she needs a change, but she's not sure what that change should be.

After the death of her parents, she decides with her sisters to move to the lake house where she has so many cherished memories from childhood, and the five of them will convert it to a bed and breakfast.

Her new home is torn up, and she needs to get re-licensed as a real estate agent in her new state. During her time off, she becomes reacquainted with the town and all of the people there.

With her sisters at her side, she attempts to forge her way in a new enterprise while finding the girl with a love of life who she lost along the way.

Come and visit Bear Lake to get to know the Romriell sisters and learn about their beautiful B&B.

ONE

Alyssa Romriell stepped out of her car into a huge puddle of slush. Salt Lake City could be beautiful, but the snow seemed never-ending on that dreary March day, and she would have done anything for sunshine. All around her were buildings covered with gray snow, and she could smell the smog.

The parking lot of her gym was being redone, and the members were being forced to park on the side of the street instead of in the parking lot they were used to, leaving the gym a virtual ghost town. Alyssa couldn't stop going, though. No, even one day off, and she started to get pudgy again. She tried to watch what she ate, but it was so much easier to do another ten minutes on the treadmill instead. Learning to be mindful about her eating was difficult, because she'd always been slender until recent years.

She took a deep breath, thinking about how very much she hated being a slave to this place. She'd always thought she was fit, with a trim waist and hips, but when she'd started dating Tim, he'd made it clear he didn't want to be seen with a woman as rotund as Alyssa. She had four sisters, and the others all commented on how thin she was, but obviously they didn't know her like Tim did.

Walking through the door, she looked around her, noting the old gym equipment and the smell of old socks that always seemed to be part of a place where *real* bodybuilders worked out. And that's where she had to exercise. She'd wanted to become a member of a posh health club where she could work out, and then sit in a sauna, and maybe a hot tub. Where she could get a massage when her muscles were a little sore.

But no. Tim had hooked her up with his friend, a personal trainer named Barbie. Barbie looked nothing like her name, though. She was built in a way that women rarely were, and her muscles had muscles. She did have blond hair like a Barbie doll, but it was cut short and spiked straight up on top of her head. And she usually had the tips colored green or blue. Never a soft, feminine color, though. There was nothing at all feminine about *this* Barbie.

"You're late!" Barbie barked at her.

Alyssa sighed. "By one minute, and only because I stepped in a bunch of cold slush when I got out of my car. Give me a minute, and I'll change into my work out clothes and be ready to go."

Barbie merely grunted at her, and Alyssa hurried to the bathroom to carry out her plan. This place didn't even have a locker room.

Alyssa changed out of her work clothes—a crisp blue skirt, a white blouse, and a blazer, complete with three-inch heels—and into a pair of sweats that were too big and an old t-shirt. She sat down and put on socks and shoes, and she was ready—physically at least.

The next hour was grueling as Barbie put Alyssa through her paces. Barbie pushed her much harder than she would ever push herself, and throughout, she heard, "You want to be strong, don't you? You won't get there if you don't *push!*"

When the hour was over, Alyssa wiped the sweat from her face and hurried into the bathroom. There were no showers, so she did a quick sponge bath with paper towels in the sink there and changed back into her work clothes. She had a date with Tim, and he expected her to look nice for him.

She brushed her hair, added a pale pink lipstick, and hurried out of the gym, waving at Barbie, who was now grunting loudly as she lifted ridiculous amounts of weight. Being a gym rat suited the other woman perfectly, and Alyssa was sure she'd never seen her in anything but shorts.

In her car, Alyssa hurried to the restaurant where she was meeting Tim, and she arrived five minutes later. Her last client had really cut into the extra time she put into her day, and now she was running late for everything. She hated being late. But she knew Tim hated her being late even more.

Tim's car was parked out front, but he wasn't in it, so she hurried into the restaurant, realizing it had started snowing again. She did her best not to slip on the ice in front of the door and noticed a man who was carefully holding the elbow of his wife or girlfriend. She wished Tim did that for her, but he expected her to be self-sufficient, and she wanted to please him.

They'd dated for more than seven years now, not long after she'd received her real estate license and started doing well. From the moment she'd gotten her license, she'd been one of the best sellers in her firm. She was very good at what she did, and she had the paychecks to prove it. Of course, she tended to be good at everything she did, and she always had been. Everything but relationships apparently, because it seemed that she was incapable of pleasing her boyfriend.

When she walked inside, she spotted Tim at a table and wove her way through the restaurant to join him. She leaned down and kissed his cheek in greeting before sitting across from him and picking up the menu. She knew from past experience that if she didn't decide what she wanted quickly, he would choose for her, and she would be having a side salad for supper. And after her workout, she needed a real meal.

Reading over the menu, she decided on a pot roast with mashed potatoes and carrots, all smothered in gravy. Tim wouldn't approve, but she'd tell him about her workout, and it would appease him. She hoped.

She set the menu down and took a drink of the water in front of her. He'd obviously already ordered drinks, because he was sipping on a Coke.

"I'm sorry I was late."

Tim shook his head. "I don't know why you can't keep better track of your time."

Alyssa sighed. She hated disappointing him. "My last client ran later than expected, but he made an offer today, which thrills me. And then, at the gym, I stepped in a huge pile of slush, and the water got into my shoe. And I think Barbie worked me for an extra five minutes, just to get back at me for being late."

"Barbie wouldn't do that. I've known her for years, and she's one of the kindest women alive." Tim speared her with his brown eyes, making her feel three inches tall.

"You've known her longer than me," Alyssa said, neither agreeing nor disagreeing with him. She couldn't agree, and she'd learned long ago not to argue. Tim was always right. She knew because he told her. Often. "How'd the job hunt go today?"

"Terrible." Tim frowned. "I swear no one in this town is hiring. Not for a man of my talents. They all want some IT guy."

Alyssa knew Tim had no desire to be an IT guy. He was a computer programmer and had once worked for a game designer. When he'd had to leave that job—he was fired due to nepotism—he had aspired to do the same thing over and over again. So far, it hadn't happened. "Maybe you could be an IT guy, just for a little while. I know you're getting behind on your bills . . ." She truly didn't understand why he didn't just take a job when it was offered. His unemployment had run out, and he needed money. Badly.

"Because it would be a step down. I don't take steps down. Only up." Tim looked angry that she'd even questioned him.

"But you're not being *offered* a step up," she said softly, hoping he'd see reason for a change.

"No, I'm not, but I should be."

The waiter came to their table then, and they each gave their order.

After their server walked away, Tim shook his head at Alyssa. "I can't believe you're putting that into your body."

"I missed lunch because I was so busy today, and then I had a pretty intense workout session. I think I can have some pot roast without putting weight on." But she was embarrassed that he was confronting her about it.

"You know better than that." He looked at her closely. "It might be time for you to try a new hair color. That shade of brunette really doesn't look good on you. It makes you look mousy."

"This is my natural color," Alyssa said softly. "Remember? We decided that I should let it grow out and become its natural color again." Well, he'd decided, and she'd capitulated. As always.

"Do what you want. I just don't think I should be expected to be seen in public with a mouse."

The waiter slid their salads in front of them, and Alyssa took her first bite eagerly. She wasn't a fan of salad, but it was food, and she was hungry. "I'll think about it."

"You do that." He forked up a bite of his own salad. "I need to borrow some money."

Alyssa immediately nodded, knowing what was expected of her. Even when he was working, she made more than double what he did. "How much?" She started to add "this time," but she had a feeling that wouldn't go over well at all.

He named a figure that she well knew was much more than his bills for a month.

"Why so much?"

"Why are you questioning me? You know I'll pay it back. I need new suits for interviews." He gestured with his fork as he talked, flinging a small amount of ranch dressing at her. He expected her to eat vinaigrettes that were healthier, but he loved ranch.

"But you just got new suits six months ago." She knew because she'd footed the bill.

He frowned. "They don't fit anymore."

She looked more closely at him, and she could see that he'd put on some weight. She couldn't mention it, because she knew how much it hurt when he mentioned her weight, so she let it go. "I see. All right. I don't have my checkbook with me, but I'll get you the money tomorrow."

"Good."

Their salad bowls were whisked away, and the entrees were placed before them. This restaurant was on the nicer side and usually one of her favorites. The night was not going well, though. She'd lost two pounds, and she had hoped he would notice and say something. Her mother certainly noticed and fussed over her whenever they saw one another.

The atmosphere was intimate, with soft jazz playing in the background. The food was good, mostly comfort food, but there were grilled chicken and fish mixed in. The aroma made her stomach sit up and pay attention.

She picked up her fork and took a bite of her pot roast, wanting to groan aloud it tasted so good. She knew it would just anger Tim, though.

When they were finished eating, he slid the check toward her to pay. She tucked her Visa into the slot in the black check folder and pushed it to the edge of the table for the waiter to pick up.

"What are your plans for the weekend?" She tried to keep her voice casual. They'd been an item for so long that he often forgot to set up plans with her, and they went days between contact at times.

"I'm going skiing with some buddies." Tim leaned back in his chair, watching her face. "No girls allowed."

"I see." Skiing was an expensive hobby of his. One of many. "I hope you have a good time."

"Oh, I will. I always do."

The waiter brought her card back, and she signed the slip, adding a tip and putting the card back into her wallet. "I think I'll have to work. There are lots of people who are interested in seeing houses this weekend." She needed to have something to do so he knew she wouldn't be sitting home alone pining for him.

They walked to their cars, and he watched as she slipped a little on the ice, catching herself at the last moment. "Be careful. It would be embarrassing for both of us if you landed on your bottom on the pavement."

When they reached his car, he kissed her briefly, and it felt as if he was going through the motions—kissing her because it was expected of him. "I'll come by your office tomorrow to pick up the money."

Alyssa nodded. "G'night, Tim."

He was already in his car and reversing out of the parking lot. She simply stood there, watching him drive away before walking to her own car and getting in. She couldn't help but wonder when he'd started going through the motions of a relationship instead of really caring about her. He had cared once, hadn't he?

After a moment, she pulled herself together and reached for the glove compartment and the emergency box of Junior Mints she always kept there. Junior Mints fixed everything.

TWO

Nick Peot dressed for work in the dark, not wanting to wake his sleeping fiancée, Kami. If she was true to form, she wouldn't get up until noon, and then she'd spend her day frittering the time away. When he got home, she would say she'd been too tired to make dinner, and he would need to take her out somewhere.

He sighed. She wasn't the woman he'd thought she was six months before when he'd asked her to marry him, and they'd moved in together.

He glanced at her in the dark. She wore a black sleep mask to block out light, and yet she still complained if he turned on a dim light to get dressed in the mornings. Her blond hair spread out over the pillow like a fan, and her face was completely relaxed. Or if it wasn't, it should be. Her twice weekly facials he paid for should keep her face as relaxed as her well-massaged body.

Nick left the room and sank down on the couch to put on his socks and boots. By the bits of sunlight streaming in through the window, he looked around the living room of the log cabin he'd built with his own hands on the weekends. It had taken him three years to finish it, but he couldn't imagine living somewhere he'd be prouder of. It was a three-bedroom, two-bath cabin, with a well-equipped kitchen. Despite the modern kitchen, it still looked as if it was something out of a historical novel. He felt good about living there, and he would build on as his family grew—if it ever did. If he was going to go through with the lavish wedding Kami was planning, then he doubted kids were even an option. She wouldn't let her figure go for something as unworthy as having his children.

He got to his feet and headed for the door. Kami complained if he "rattled around in the kitchen" in the mornings making himself breakfast, so he'd stop at a Maverik along the way. They didn't have his first choice in breakfasts, but they had something that would work for him.

As he drove to nearby Garden City, Utah from the tiny town of Richland, Idaho, where he'd been born and raised, his thoughts were still on Kami and his dreadful situation with her. He needed to break things off—and soon—but he knew she was going to turn on the water works. Kami wasn't a girl who cried naturally, he'd learned. She just turned on the tears when they suited whatever situation she was in. She manipulated people with her tears, plain and simple.

Nick felt terrible even having these thoughts about the woman he was supposed to marry, but after several months of her doing nothing to even clean the house, he had gotten to this point. He worked all week, went home every day to take her out to dinner, and he spent his weekends catching up on cleaning and doing laundry. If he wanted anything done, he had to do it himself, which wasn't how he'd seen her being a stay-at-home wife going. He was sure now that she had started the way she'd meant them to go on after marriage.

He stopped for a breakfast burrito at the Maverik before he moved onto the jobsite. He was doing a bathroom renovation on a lake house in Garden City. The job would take about two weeks for him to do, and then he'd have to find something else. Summer was coming, and since people tended to spend more time at the lake in the summers, they didn't usually want to have work done then. Summers were lean for a building contractor in the area, and he'd often have to drive out farther. The best he could hope for would be building a deck, because people understood that *had* to be done in summer months.

When he got to the job, the lady of the house was waiting for him. "Good morning, Nick. What's on the agenda today?" She was wearing a skimpy nightgown, as she had every morning to see him. It was still winter, and she had to be freezing. He was sure she wore normal clothes while her husband was there, and then ran off to change as soon as the man left. He couldn't imagine why she did the things she did.

"Just finishing up the new flooring in the bathroom, and I'll start on the tile around the tub tomorrow. I think you're really going to like that new bathtub I just put in." He didn't look at her as he spoke.

Mrs. Simmons took a step closer to him, trailing one finger down the front of his shirt. "I'm sure I will. It looks big enough for two."

"I'm an engaged man, Mrs. Simmons." And there. That's why he couldn't break off his engagement for another week or two. He had to have a reason to get away from her.

"And I'm a married woman. I don't mind if you don't mind." She smiled up at him in a way that made his blood curdle. The woman wasn't the least bit attractive to him, because he hated cheating so much.

"I mind." He stepped back from her and turned toward the bathroom. "I need to get to work."

She sighed, obviously annoyed he wouldn't capitulate. He wasn't quite sure why she kept trying every single day, but she did.

By lunchtime, Nick had worked out a plan. He would finish the job he was working, and then he would let Kami know that he was breaking things off. He'd take a few days between jobs to help her pack up her things and get settled somewhere else. It was only right that he at least tried to help her start a new life without him.

Having a plan in place helped him know that he was doing the right thing. Soon she'd be out of his hair, and he was sure she'd be in someone else's pretty darn quick. It was just the kind of woman she was.

When he got home from work that day, there was no supper cooking—as usual—and Kami was waiting on the couch for him, already dressed for supper in a short skirt and low-cut blouse. How he'd ever thought he wanted to marry someone like her truly escaped him.

"Hurry and change. I made reservations for supper at six-thirty, and you're going to make us late."

Not wanting to start an argument, he went into the master bath to shower and change. He put on jeans and a polo, knowing she wouldn't find it dressy enough, but it was about as dressy as he got, except for special occasions. She'd just have to learn to make compromises until he ended things with her. Just a couple more weeks.

He walked into the living room and smiled to himself. He was counting down the days.

THREE

On Saturday morning, Alyssa did her usual weekend errands, hitting the grocery store first. She knew she was going to have a rough weekend, so she grabbed two tubs of Junior Mint ice cream, having no problem envisioning herself eating it straight from the carton.

As she walked up and down each aisle of the store, she longed for a quieter life. When she'd been a girl, she had spent two weeks every summer and every weekend of the summer at Bear Lake, which was on the border of Utah and Idaho. Her parents still owned a lake house there, and she briefly wondered if she should go and spend some time there, but as soon as the thought crossed her mind, she received a phone call from one of her favorite clients.

"I have some free time today I didn't expect. Do you have time to take me to a few more houses I found?" Karl Schmidt asked her. He was one of her biggest clients and was looking for a vacation home that was a little closer to the Park City, Utah area. Normally she didn't go that far out, but she was happy to do it for such a good client.

"I always have free time for you," she answered automatically. "I can meet you at my office in an hour." Alyssa would have to cut her shopping trip short and finish up buying what she needed later, but she'd have enough time to check out, get home and put her groceries away, and change into work clothes before meeting him.

"That sounds good. Thanks, Alyssa."

She hurried toward the front of the store, knowing she wanted the commission he'd be bringing in. As she stood in line, she bought three more boxes of emergency Junior Mints to put into her glove compartment. With the way things were going with Tim, she knew she'd need them.

An hour later, she was dressed and at her office. Thankfully, Mr. Schmidt wasn't there yet, and she had time to just sit for a moment, reflecting on her terrible night on Thursday. She wasn't sure what had gotten into Tim lately, but she knew that he wasn't the man he used to be. Or maybe he just wasn't the man he used to *seem* to be.

She spotted Mr. Schmidt walking toward her, and he got into the passenger side of her car. "Thanks for agreeing to meet me. I know you probably had other plans for your weekend."

Alyssa genuinely liked the older man. He wasn't as snooty as most of the rich people she knew were. He was actually always thankful when she took him around.

"I'm so happy to do it. Which houses do you want to look at this time?" This was their fourth trip to the Park City area, and he always had a specific house or two in mind when they went to look.

He gave her the addresses, and she plugged the first into her GPS. She knew the houses had come from listings that she'd sent him for the area, and she hoped this time they'd find the one he considered perfect for his family. He was in his late fifties, a widower with several grandkids. He wanted a place where his entire family could spend a couple of weeks together every summer. Just like she'd had with her family growing up.

As she drove, he regaled her with tales about his twin grandsons, who were apparently perfect in every way, and she listened and laughed at the funny parts, even though she had no desire to laugh.

Being a real estate agent meant that she needed to be on whenever she was with a client.

The first house they looked at had Mr. Schmidt excited. "This is what I'm looking for."

Alyssa pulled up all the information she had on the house and told him what she could as they walked. "The house is only five years old. The people who owned it before have decided they want to be at a lake and not the mountains. So, you benefit from their mind change." She led him up a flight of stairs. "This is the master suite. It has a huge bathtub with separate shower. There are four other bedrooms on this level and two on the main level. You have three children?" she asked.

He nodded. "That's perfect, too, because then each of my children can have a room with their spouse, and the grandkids for each family can have their own room."

"Sounds smart to me."

They looked in closets and cabinets as they moved along.

When they were finished looking at the downstairs rooms and the kitchen, he grinned. "I don't even need to see the other place. The hot tub out back is staying, right?"

"Yes, it is. So is the sauna."

"I'm taking it. Where do I sign?"

Alyssa smiled, pulling a contract out of her purse. She kept one on her at all times for just such an occasion. "Let's get this filled out. Do you know what you want to offer?"

In less than thirty minutes, they were back on the road and headed to her office in North Salt Lake. She lived and worked out of North Salt Lake, but most of her business tended to be in Salt Lake City. It was also where she worked out.

"Thanks for sticking with me through all of my shopping," he told her. "I think I would have driven anyone else crazy. I hope I'll be given a chance to review my experience with you."

"I have honestly enjoyed it, Mr. Schmidt. You made it easy for me." And he had. Very easy.

After Alyssa dropped him off, she went into her office and did the paperwork on the sale, wanting to dance a little jig. The commission on the house would be good, but better than that, she'd found a vacation home for a wonderful man who would use it to make special memories for his grandkids. Memories like the ones she had of her family's lake house.

When she'd finished filing the paperwork, she went back to the grocery store to continue her shopping trip. She didn't use a list and couldn't remember what she'd purchased, and she knew she would be doubling up on a few things. It was all right, though. She knew it would get eaten or donated. She often bought things she never ended up using, but food pantries were there for a reason.

She bought all the stuff she needed to make her recipe for shepherd's pie for supper. She had tried dozens of recipes, and what she'd finally kept was parts of about six of them plus her own twist.

The woman at the checkout was familiar to her, but not someone she knew by name, or who knew her by name, which had her once again thinking about the simpler lifestyle in Richland, where she'd spent lots of time every summer on Bear Lake. A couple of years, she and her sisters had spent the entire summer at the lake, and her father —a dentist who specialized in TMJ—would spend four days a week working, and then he'd join them Friday through Sunday. Those had been the summers she'd liked the best. She treasured the memory of them.

On her way home, she ran through Chick-fil-A for chicken nuggets and a frozen lemonade. It was what she needed—along with her Junior Mint ice cream—to make it through the weekend. She had some serious thinking to do about her relationship with Tim and decisions to make about what she wanted to do.

She plopped down on the couch and reached for the remote, planning to watch some of her favorite rom-coms on her large flat-screen television. The walls were a pale blue, and the décor was different shades of the same color, with some white thrown in for accents. It was a cozy, feminine room which she always felt comfortable in. Spending time there and eating Junior Mints were always her solutions for having hard days. And they always seemed to work.

She had her remote in hand and the ice cream and a spoon on the coffee table in front of her when her phone rang. Glancing at the display, she saw that it was Hannah, her childhood best friend who had been raised in Richland, right there on the lake.

"Hello!" Alyssa hadn't realized just how much she needed to hear her friend's voice until that very moment.

"Hey, you!" Hannah's voice sounded as sweet as ever. "I hadn't heard from you in a while, so I figured I'd catch up. I have about thirty minutes between jobs today."

"I've been busy," Alyssa said by way of apology. "Tell me what's going on in your world."

Hannah sighed. "The usual. I'm working days at the grocery store. Nights at Coopers over in Fish Haven. And weekends are spent cleaning houses. I'm going to have that bookstore saved for in another thirteen months. Do you believe? It's almost time. And I'm going to run the best bookstore the Bear Lake Valley has ever seen! Just you wait."

"I know you will. You're amazing." Alyssa couldn't imagine working all those menial jobs simply so she could open a bookstore, but she'd been raised very differently than Hannah had. Her friend had always had to work for everything she wanted, while Alyssa had been handed the world. She wasn't sure which was better, but she wished her friend would allow her to invest in her business so she could slow down a little.

"Well, thank you very much. No one can make me feel quite as good about myself as you do."

Alyssa smiled. "That goes double for me. Are you seeing anyone?"

Hannah laughed. "Like I have time to see someone. I work a ridiculous number of hours and never take a day off. Who would I meet working so much? And where would I find the time to date him?"

"Just asking! I think it would do you good to slow down a little. Remember, I'd love to invest . . ."

"Nope. Thanks, though." The answer was quick. "So, how's it going with Tim?"

Alyssa didn't miss the annoyance in her friend's voice when she said Tim's name. "He's . . . strange."

"Always has been in my opinion . . . but what makes you think now is any different from always?"

Alyssa laughed a little, shaking her head. She needed some face-to-face time with Hannah, and not the kind that came from Skype or Facetime. Real friend time. A short conversation was all she needed to know that. She missed her friend. "He's just acting oddly. He kissed me goodnight the last time I saw him, and he didn't put any real . . . feeling behind it, if that makes sense. It was just a cursory kiss because he was supposed to. And I asked him what he was doing this weekend, and he's spending the weekend with guy friends, because he wants to ski, but he told me it was a men's only weekend, like I was going to try to infringe on his plans."

"And who is paying for this ski weekend? Isn't he still unemployed?"

Alyssa sighed. "He said he'd pay me back . . ." She was tired of the constant drain he was on her finances, just like her friend, but . . . she had so much time vested in the relationship. She couldn't give up on Tim now, could she?

"Of course, he did. He always says that." Hannah sighed dramatically, and Alyssa could just picture her rolling her eyes. "I wish you'd dump that jerk and just move on with your life."

"Would you be able to give up a seven-year relationship just like that? I feel like I should stay with him just a little bit longer. I'm sure he'll get a job soon, and he'll be back to normal."

"Alyssa, you know as well as I do that the man is *not* normal. Not even one little bit. He loves himself, and there's no room for him to love anyone else. He's using your money to go on a vacation that he told you you're not allowed to go on. He's got you all messed up in your thinking about your weight—which is perfect, by the way. It was perfect *before* you started dating him!"

"I know. I know." But she didn't. She looked in a mirror, and she could see that she needed to lose weight. A significant amount of weight actually. And Tim told her the same thing, so he had to be right, didn't he? "I'm just not ready to make any drastic changes to my life."

"I understand that. I also know it's time. And I don't need to yell at you about it. You'll figure it out on your own soon enough. And I have to go. Third housecleaning job of the day. Just remind me one more time that I'm doing this for all the right reasons. I'm going to be surrounded by books!"

Alyssa laughed softly. "That's been your dream for as long as I can remember."

"It really has. And I'm going to make it happen. Bye. Love you, and I want you to come stay in your parents' lake house soon! It's been forever." With that, Hannah ended the call, and Alyssa sat staring at her phone for a moment.

Was Hannah right? Was it really time to end a relationship that she'd had forever? How could it be time? After seven long years, she should get something out of the relationship, shouldn't she? They'd talked marriage. A little voice asked her if she wanted to raise children with someone like Tim, but she didn't let herself think about it too much. She couldn't. Not yet.

Alyssa shook her head. She was being melodramatic and silly. Reaching for the remote, she switched on *Notting Hill* before reaching for her ice cream and a spoon. She was sure the ice cream would make everything clear, and she'd know exactly what she needed to do. Junior Mints fixed the world, and when they were in ice cream, their power was multiplied.

She dug her spoon into the carton, not bothering with a bowl, as she watched Julia Roberts walk into a bookstore in *Notting Hill.* She sighed as she lost herself in the romance of the movie. She'd figure things out later.

FOUR

Friday afternoon, Nick left work a little early, hoping to be able to fix supper himself and save a little money. Besides, Mrs. Simmons was coming on stronger than ever, and he needed to stay away from her. There was no excuse for cheating. Ever. He wasn't going to be the one to help her cheat on her husband, and he wasn't going to cheat on Kami, even though she already had a foot out the door without knowing it. He would stay true to her until the day he officially broke it off.

He stopped at the grocery store—another household chore that Kami avoided like the plague—and grabbed some ground beef, some spaghetti sauce, a loaf of garlic bread, and a bag of spaghetti noodles. He knew Kami would complain if wine wasn't involved in their meal, but he didn't like wine, and he wasn't about to buy it if he didn't like it. He was finished pandering to the girl.

When he got to the front, he smiled at the checker at the register he chose. "Hi, Hannah. How's things?"

"Oh, busy as usual. How're things with you? And Kami?"

He shrugged. "Mostly okay. I'm staying busy, and Kami isn't." He hadn't meant to say the words, and he wanted to clamp his hand over his mouth as soon as they escaped, but he didn't. They were true.

Hannah just grinned as she quickly rang up his purchases. The store was small and fit the town perfectly. He could walk in, go exactly where he needed to go, and buy everything he needed in five minutes flat. A full-on grocery trip took a little longer, but only about fifteen minutes. There wasn't a huge selection, but there was food, and he could get it quick. That made up for the lack of selection in his eyes. Besides, if he wanted a bigger store, he could drive over to Montpelier or even to Logan in Utah.

She gave him the price, and he pulled out a debit card.

"How are your parents?" Hannah asked as he swiped the card and went through the questions the card reader asked.

"They're good. They're in Tuscon now, living the retired dream."

"Sounds like my folks. Mom is pestering Dad to get a condo in Florida, and Dad thinks it's a waste of money. They argue about it constantly." Hannah handed him his receipt. "I'd say 'Come again,' but I know you will." She winked at him. They both knew they were friendly and there would never be anything more between them, and they were both happy with that fact.

He laughed. "Always. Have a good day, and I'm sure I'll see you soon!"

Hannah nodded, smiling as she moved onto the next customer.

Nick thought a lot of Hannah, knowing she worked three jobs to try and make her dream come true. She had been working three jobs since she graduated from high school, and it wore him out just thinking about the sheer number of hours she had to work. He couldn't imagine having to work that way, but if he had children, he guessed he would do what it took to feed them. Still, it was a hard way to live.

He put the food into the front seat of his truck and started the engine. He wasn't looking forward to Kami's annoyance at him cooking dinner and not taking her out. He wasn't sure why anyone would want to eat out every night of the week, but Kami did.

When he pulled into his driveway, there was a car he didn't recognize. He looked at it for a moment, noting the Utah plates and the car seat in the back. It was a small-sized SUV and looked like it was made for hauling children around. Nick couldn't think of a single friend of Kami's who had small children, but he certainly didn't mind her having friends over.

There was still snow covering the shrubs he'd planted on either side of the driveway, and the trees all had a light dusting. The snow was deep in front of the house, but he'd painstakingly removed it using a four-wheeler equipped with a snow plow. His driveway was long, and he didn't think he could shovel it all. Well, he knew he could, but it would be hard work.

Nick opened the door and noticed the lights were off, which was odd. If Kami was entertaining someone, she should be with them in the living room, shouldn't she? He put the groceries on the counter and walked through the house to the master bedroom, where he could hear low voices. Pushing the door open, he stopped where he was, in shock.

Kami was in bed with a man he didn't know.

He cleared his throat. "When you're finished, I'd like to talk to you, Kami." He was surprised he didn't feel hurt by it. After all, they'd been together for two years. All he felt was relief. He could get rid of her now, and he wouldn't even feel an ounce of guilt for it.

He closed the door and walked back to the kitchen, intent on cooking his supper. She wouldn't be eating it with him as planned, but he was still going to enjoy his meal—the first meal he'd eaten at home in a good long while.

He was just finishing up browning the meat when Kami walked into the kitchen, wrapped in a bathrobe. "I guess you finished? Did you tell your friend to leave?" Nick asked, not bothering to give her more than a cursory glance.

She sighed. "I did. I'm sorry you had to catch us that way, but a woman has needs. You should have been treating me like a princess and making love to me every night instead of being so worried about your career." She crossed her arms over her chest, obviously ready for a fight.

He looked at her then, wondering what he'd ever seen in her. Her blond hair was obviously from a bottle, though she still denied it. She always seemed to think she was better than the people around her, and he got sick of apologizing for her. No, there were no feelings left inside him for her. "So, I was planning on finishing the job I'm working and taking a few days off to pack and help you get out of my house. You've saved me the trouble. Leave. Now."

"You can't mean that, Nick. I know you love me." She stepped closer to him, pressing herself against him.

All he felt was disgust. She hadn't even showered after having sex with someone else, and she was trying to offer herself to him? He put his hands on her shoulders and gently pushed her away from him. "No. I don't. Leave. I'll pack your things up this weekend and put them on the doorstep Monday morning before I leave for work. If anything is still here when I get home Monday evening, I'll burn it. Every last thing."

Her face flushed with anger, her eyes narrowing. "You can't do this to me! Where am I supposed to go?"

"Your parents live thirty minutes from here. Your lover in there can take you home with him. I really don't care where you go, Kami, as long as I don't have to put up with you for another minute."

"What are you doing home early anyway?" she asked, tapping her foot with her arms tightly crossed against her chest. She obviously wasn't giving up without a fight.

Nick saw the man she'd been in bed with flee the house, and he chuckled. "Look at that. Your lover boy was afraid I'd hurt him over you. Not happening. You don't matter enough for me to fight anyone."

Kami raised a hand to slap him, but he caught it in the air before it connected.

"You're a cold-hearted jerk."

He shook his head. "Go away, Kami. I'm tired of looking at you."

He dropped her hand and turned to drain the grease off his meat into a coffee can he kept for just such a purpose. He had no need to speak with her again. She just needed to do as she was told for once in her miserable life.

"What about the wedding invitations? They're already out!"

He didn't even respond as he filled a pot with hot water and put it on to boil. She could deal with the invitations. She could show up for the wedding for all he cared, but he wasn't spending another dime on it, and he wouldn't be there. He preheated the oven for the garlic bread and added the sauce to the meat. He'd start packing right after supper. He whistled as he finished seasoning the pasta sauce and walked around to sit on one of the barstools he'd carved out of an old oak tree. Everything in his cabin was handmade and of the best quality. And she was throwing it—and him—away. Good riddance to her.

"Nick, please, if you'll just listen to me."

He pulled the air pods he used while he worked from his pocket and stuck them in his ears, hearing the audio book he'd been listening to come through the speakers loudly and clearly.

Finally, Kami got the hint, and she hurried off to change into real clothes and get out of his house. At least that's what he hoped she was doing. He wasn't putting up with any more of her nonsense, and if she came back out in her robe, Nick was going to throw her out in the snow still wearing it. It wouldn't hurt him even a little bit to do so.

Thankfully, he didn't have to go to that extreme, and she stomped out into the hallway, glaring at him. She said something to him, but he couldn't hear it over his book, and he watched as she left with a small suitcase and the clothes on her back.

He picked up his phone and called the grocery store, hearing his book pause and the call go into his AirPods. "I need some moving boxes? Do you have any extra lying around?"

"Nick?" the voice asked.

"Hannah? Yeah, it's Nick. Kami's moving out, and I need to pack her stuff up this weekend before she gets back."

There was silence for a moment. "We have boxes. Come and get them when you're ready."

"I'll be there as soon as I finish eating. Thanks. Make sure someone knows I'm coming." Nick was sure she was leaving for the day. It was time for her second job.

"I will. I'm about to head to Coopers, so I'll make sure the manager gives them to you. Sorry. I hoped she was the one for you."

Nick smiled at the friendliness. He had tried dating Hannah once in school, but neither of them had felt anything for the other. He thought they were probably too much alike for things to work out between them. They'd stayed friends, though, and he was glad. "Thanks. I already knew she was not the woman I was looking for, but I appreciate the sympathy." With those words, he ended the call and went to check on his spaghetti. He was hungry, and he was going to enjoy his meal, no matter what kind of chaos was going on around him.

FIVE

Alyssa finished her last showing of the day, and because she had no plans for the weekend, she went to the grocery store so she could spend the entire weekend at home, ensconced in front of the fire, watching movies. Or maybe she'd re-binge watch something. That was always fun.

As she was looking at the different cheeses, trying to decide which one to have with crackers and summer sausage over the weekend, her phone rang, and she pulled it out. She half-hoped it was a client who wanted to see something over the weekend so she wouldn't feel so dreadfully alone, but instead, it was her mother.

"Hey, Mom. What's happening in your world?"

Her mother's voice was sweet and soothing, and Alyssa always felt better after talking to her. She was definitely closer to her mother than she was her father. All of her sisters felt like they were closer to their dad, but not her. She'd take her mother any day of the week.

"I just wanted to let you know that your father and I are going up to the lake for the weekend."

"Oh, that's awesome." Alyssa considered asking to go with them for a moment, but she decided against it. She needed to be on call for her clients. "If you run into Hannah, give her a big hug for me."

"You know I will. Oh, and I have a professional question . . ."

Alyssa smiled. That was the real reason her mother was calling. She didn't usually check in with her daughters when she wanted to spend some time out of town. There was no need, as they were all adults. Only Lauren still lived at home, and that was because she'd just graduated from college in December. With a liberal arts degree, no less. What was she supposed to do with a liberal arts degree? Alyssa had offered her a job working for her, but she'd have to get her real estate license, and Lauren was sure she didn't want to do sales. What else could she do with a liberal arts degree, though?

"I'm here to be your real estate expert." She found the cheese she wanted and dumped it in the cart, moving down to get some skim milk to eat over her cereal. Crunch Berries were in order, and she didn't care at all what Tim thought about it.

"I'm so glad, because I don't have any other daughters with your expertise." There was amusement in her mother's voice, and that thrilled Alyssa. Her mother had the best sense of humor, and she was so drawn to it. "We're thinking about selling the lake house. We only make it up there every few months, and we're paying more for maintenance than we're getting use out of it. What do you think it's worth?"

"No!" Alyssa couldn't imagine losing the house where she had so many wonderful memories. She could close her eyes and picture sitting on the front porch swing or having a water balloon fight on the back deck while her father grilled burgers for them for supper. She could see the fireworks display they had always watched from the yard, put on right there in Richland. It would break her heart to not have the house available to them.

"Alyssa, none of you girls have been to the lake house in at least three years. Why would we keep it when there's another family who can buy it and make the same kind of happy memories we have in it?"

"I guess I just like knowing it's there, so I can go whenever I want to." Someone reached around her for butter, because she'd stopped in the middle of the aisle, unable to move any farther. She moved out of the way, but she couldn't keep shopping. Not while talking about *this*.

"I know. But it's not logical or economical. Your dad and I are thinking about getting a condo in Arizona. It's time we were in a warmer climate."

Alyssa closed her eyes against the tears. *Not the lake house. Anything but the lake house.* "It's probably worth between five hundred to six hundred thousand, depending on the market at the lake. Do you want me to find a real estate agent to help you with the sale?"

"That would be really nice, if you don't mind. I know it's not what you want, but I think it's what your father and I *need.* We'll spend summers at the house in Kaysville and winters in Arizona. Or maybe Florida. We're thinking of looking near Disney because when the grandbabies start coming, we'll want to be able to take them. Hint hint."

Alyssa laughed softly. "When do you leave for the lake?"

"We're on the road now. Go ahead and text me the name of the real estate agent, because you know how bad service is between here and the lake."

"All right. It's no problem." But it was. It really was. *The lake house.*

Alyssa tucked her phone back into her purse and continued her shopping trip, but now all she could think about was the lake house. About the beautiful little town of Richland, Idaho and how very much she missed it.

As she checked out, she thought about seeing a friendly face at the register like she would have in Richland. Maybe it was time for her to visit the lake house. One last weekend with all of them there before the house sold. They could pack and cry and reminisce. She felt like a part of her childhood was being sold—the most important part.

When she got home, she found the name of a real estate agent for her mother and texted it to her, not wanting to help but not wanting to stand in her parents' way either. She was so conflicted about the whole thing. Couldn't they rent it out weekly for vacationers and use it when they wanted? There had to be other options than selling. It was too *important* to sell.

Alyssa ate an entire box of Junior Mints, calling her sister, Taylor, who was two years younger than her. "Hey, Taylor. Did Mom call you?"

"No . . . why would Mom call me?" Taylor asked, sounding confused.

"She called me to ask for the name of a real estate agent in Idaho. They're selling the lake house." Alyssa had no doubt her sister would feel the same way she did. They'd shared too much in that house.

"No!"

Alyssa heard the same panic in her sister's voice that she'd felt herself. "Yup. She says we never use it, and they want to move to Arizona or Florida."

"Way to be clichéd retired people, Mom and Dad." Taylor was quiet for a moment. "They're really going to sell?"

"Mom asked me what I thought they'd get for it and asked for a name. She said they're spending one last weekend and talking to someone about selling. I don't want to see it go."

"I don't either. I want to sit here and cry."

"Well, depending on where you are, that's not a terrible thing to do. I was in the grocery store when she told me." Alyssa shook her head. "I wanted to sit down in the middle of the aisle and bawl like a baby. I did cause something of a traffic jam in the dairy section."

"I'm at work." Taylor was a hotel manager for a swanky hotel in downtown Salt Lake City.

"Well, you probably shouldn't cry, then. You don't want to scare the guests away."

"Oh, I want to scare some of them away," Taylor responded.

"Hang on." Alyssa listened to hold music for a minute before her sister came back on the line. "Sorry."

"No, I'm sorry. I shouldn't have kept you on the phone so long while you were at work. I'll call you when I know more. And you need to help me work on Mom and Dad. I think if we all show an interest in the house and going up there, they'll change their minds. They *have* to."

"You call the others. We'll all get together and make a plan. Save the lake house!"

Alyssa smiled. Taylor always made plans, and they were usually viable. "Save the lake house!"

After she ended the call, Alyssa called her other sisters one by one. Next, she called Amanda. "Hey, have you talked to Mom and Dad?"

"Not recently. I mean, I talk to Mom every weekend. Why? Did something happen to them?"

"Not at all. They're just thinking about selling the lake house."

"Not the lake house!" Amanda practically shouted. "Well, that was unprofessional. I'm finishing up a job. I'm just glad my clients aren't home!" Amanda was an interior decorator, and she'd done Alyssa's house. She made everything feel so homey for her, which was exactly what Alyssa had needed. Alyssa often recommended her to clients looking for decorating help.

"That's what Taylor said. Me too, actually. Taylor thinks we all need to get together and make a plan to talk them out of selling. You up for it?"

"As long as you're hosting. Your house is the biggest."

"Absolutely. I'll even make some snacks, and we'll have a sister party." Alyssa loved the idea of her lonely weekend being filled with her sisters and plans for keeping the lake house.

"Sounds good. How's two?" Amanda asked.

"I'll text Taylor and see. I think she's the only one who might be working this weekend."

"Sounds like a plan. I'll bring soft drinks. You still drink Coke?"

Alyssa thought for a moment. She *should* drink Diet Coke, but she didn't like the taste. "Yeah, Coke sounds good."

"Okay. See you tomorrow!"

"Bye."

Alyssa started a list of what she needed from the grocery store if she was making snacks for her sisters. An impromptu sister party might be just what she needed. The others could call it a planning meeting, but for Alyssa, it felt like a party.

She texted Taylor and got an immediate response that two was fine, so she went ahead with her other sisters.

She called Kayla next, just going through the order of their births. When her sister answered the phone, Alyssa could hear the sound of power tools in the background. "Yeah!"

"Hey, Kayla. I can hear you're still at work, so I'll be quick. Mom and Dad are planning to sell the lake house, and we're having a planning meeting at my house at two tomorrow afternoon to find a way to stop them. You in?"

"Absolutely. They can't sell the lake house!"

"I agree. See you tomorrow."

Alyssa called Lauren—the youngest—last. She was sure her sister knew of the plans because she was living with their parents again, but she'd find out.

"Hey, Alyssa. What's up?"

"So did Mom tell you they're planning to sell the lake house?" Alyssa asked with no preamble.

"No. She told me they were thinking about it but not that they'd decided for sure. I suggested they go up for a weekend, because I figured all the memories would crash down on them and they'd change their minds."

"Mom asked me for the name of a real estate agent there today, so it doesn't sound like they're changing their minds. They plan to go through with it."

"Ugh. I don't *want* them to sell the lake house!"

"Neither do I! So, here's what we're going to do . . ." Alyssa told Lauren what their plans were. "Does that work?"

"Yes. I'll be there." Lauren sounded as determined as the rest of them to change their parents' plans. Selling the lake house was not an option. Not for any of them.

Alyssa jotted a few more things on her list and got to her feet, heading straight back to the grocery store. They would have a lake house saving party instead of wallowing. Now that she had a course of action, she was ready to once again be part of Team Romriell Sisters and save the lake house.

SIX

NICK SPENT all day Saturday boxing up Kami's things. He was so glad to be rid of her that he didn't even feel sad. Relief was the only word that came to his mind.

His friend Ryan came over just before suppertime, and he stared at him for a moment. "Why are you building a bonfire on your front lawn? Don't you know you can't have bonfires until after the snow melts?"

"You heard, didn't you?" Nick asked. His friend wasn't fooling him one bit.

Ryan shrugged, his dark hair flopping over his forehead, and he pushed it back with an annoyed gesture. His hair was always flopping into his eyes. "I did. Kami came into the store today, pleading with me to get you to take her back. She said she made one little mistake, and you couldn't stay mad at her about it."

Nick laughed. "I'd already decided to kick her to the curb when I walked in on her with some dude in my bed. That's *not* one little mistake. That's a monumental mistake, and the woman needs to be tarred and feathered."

"I figured it was something like that. You're not the type to just kick her out. Even though I thought you should have done it years ago."

"So, I'm throwing all the pictures of the two of us together into a fire, and I figured I'd burn some old logs and enjoy myself. I might even make s'mores." Nick shrugged. "I'm thinking about throwing all the bedding the two of them used on there too."

"You know there's three feet of snow out there, don't you?"

"I guess I could do it in my burn barrel, but the dramatic flair of making a bonfire in the middle of winter really appeals to me."

Ryan laughed. "Well, as long as it appeals to you . . ."

"You wanna help?"

"What I want is to go out with my buddy tonight. We can shoot darts over at Max's Tavern. It's been a million years since we've done something like that. Kami never wanted me around, and she sure didn't want to spend an evening without you. Clingy little . . ."

"I can fill in the gaps," Nick said. "Yeah, let's do it. I haven't shot darts in a while. And maybe a game of pool! Does the tavern still make the best chicken fingers in all of Idaho?" He realized that he hadn't been there since he'd started dating Kami two years prior. It was time for him to go to a place he enjoyed with his friend.

"Sure does." Ryan grabbed Nick's coat from the closet and threw it at him, shrugging into his own. "I'm glad you dumped her. It'll be nice to have my buddy back."

"Sure will." Nick locked up with a new key. He'd changed the locks first thing that morning. Thankfully, he'd had an extra lock on his truck, because he hadn't wanted to face Ryan, who had always been quietly disapproving of Kami. And Ryan owned the only hardware store for thirty minutes in every direction. Besides, he wasn't about to give his business to the hardware store in Montpelier when he could give it to his friend. "So, how's business these days?"

As Nick drove toward the tavern, the two men caught up on each other's lives.

"I'm working for the Simmons couple. In Garden City. Mrs. Simmons will not quit coming onto me." Nick described some of the awkward conversations he'd had with Mrs. Simmons in the past few weeks. "I'd decided to keep Kami around until I finished the job, and then I was getting rid of her. It was easy to say, 'I'm an engaged man,' to get her off my back."

Ryan laughed. "Mrs. Simmons, huh? She's always seemed a little too wild for her husband."

"Oh, trust me. That's very true." Nick shook his head. "I guess I'll just have to keep reminding her that she's married and tell her I don't believe in cheating." Which was of course true. He just hadn't wanted to have to go there with the sex-crazed woman.

"So, what's lined up next?"

"I wasn't lining up another job so I could help Kami pack when I kicked her out. I guess that plan is gone, and I need to find something. If you hear of anyone looking to have a remodel done, you just let me know. I'll handle it."

Ryan nodded. "I'll keep my eyes and ears open. I always hear when someone wants something done. Well, usually I hear them complaining that they can't do it themselves first, but you know I'll turn them onto you as fast as I can."

"I appreciate it." Nick pulled into the parking lot of Max's, and they both got out, stomping through the snow that was falling on them. "First food, then darts, and then pool. I'm going to kick your butt at all of it."

Ryan laughed. "You're rusty, old man. I'd be surprised if you could figure out which end of a pool stick to use to hit the ball."

The tavern was more than fifty years old, but it had changed hands in recent years, and the outside had seen a fresh coat of paint. Inside, the barstools had been reupholstered with a green fabric, and the darts had been added. There were now televisions in every corner of the place, and there was always a sports game on. Not many women went there, because it wasn't geared toward women. It certainly wasn't a fancy nightclub. Instead it was a place for men to kick back together and enjoy their evenings after a hard day. Nick had done most of the work alongside their friend, Max. It had definitely been worth the effort, now that he could use it.

Nick was greeted by many old friends, most of whom had no idea he'd broken it off with Kami, and he had no desire to tell them any differently. They plopped down at the bar and ordered, each of them getting a soft drink. Ryan's parents had been killed by a drunk driver in high school, and Ryan had moved in with Nick's family. They'd both promised they would never drink, and to Nick's knowledge, neither of them had ever broken the promise.

The tavern wasn't a place where the tourists came, and that was nice for both men. They enjoyed their time together, playing games, eating, and hanging out with other locals.

Max came out from behind the bar and threw darts with them until the place got busy and he had to actually work. The three of them had gone to school together, and Nick considered Max one of his closest friends. Everyone in town was thankful for the money that the tourists brought to the economy, but they were glad to see them go.

When they switched to shooting pool, they started talking wagers.

"Loser has to finish packing up all those boxes."

"Worse. Loser has to sleep with Kami!" Nick said, a grin on his face.

"Oh, that's low. Good thing her brother's not here."

"Like her brother is ever in town. He moved to Logan to get rid of the small-town feel. So did her parents. I hope she stays there with them." Nick really didn't want to see Kami all over town. He didn't want to have to deal with her anymore. Why should he? The engagement was broken, and he had washed his hands of her.

An old friend of Nick's named Peter heard the way they were talking. "You broke things off with Kami?" he asked.

Nick nodded. "It was time."

"I'm sure it was. Glad you got rid of her finally. The stories I hear about the men who came and went from your house . . . I swear the woman must've been paid for her favors."

"And you didn't think to tell me?" Nick wasn't sure what kind of friend would keep something like that to himself.

"I didn't think you'd believe me."

"Well, I believe you today. I found her in bed with another man when I went home a little early yesterday. I guess she's been playing me for a fool for longer than I'd guessed."

Peter shook his head. "Most men have a blind spot when it comes to girls like Kami. They have two sides, and only one of them is real. You never saw the real side of her."

"I know." Nick thought about what his friend had said as he played the next game, though, feeling as if he'd been played for a fool.

On the drive back to his cabin, Nick asked Ryan, "Did you know she was cheating on me?"

Ryan shook his head. "I heard rumors, but I didn't put any stock in them. If I'd known, I'd have told you. I promise you that."

"I know you would have. Thanks for getting me out of the house tonight. That was exactly what I needed. A 'Kami is finally gone' celebration. It was high time it happened."

After he was alone, Nick packed up the rest of Kami's things and piled the boxes neatly in front of the door. He'd carry them all out onto the front porch before work on Monday and pray for snow.

SEVEN

THE PARTY with Alyssa's sisters went well on Saturday, and they came up with a good solid plan for what to do to keep their parents from selling. At first, it was mostly joking around.

Suggestions like one of them getting pregnant—even though unmarried—so their parents would have grandbabies to play with at the lake abounded. Lauren said she would blockade herself in the lake house and never leave. Kayla offered to make the house a construction zone, and Amanda said she could redecorate to make the house completely unappealing. They discussed the merits of each suggestion as if they were serious, until one of them couldn't help but burst into laughter. It made for an uproarious time.

Finally, they decided to talk to their parents about putting the house on Airbnb so they would all still be able to use it when they wanted. They could hire someone to clean and maintain the lawn, but their parents wouldn't be out money for it. Not that money was a huge issue for them. Even now that their father had retired from his TMJ practice, they didn't have to pinch every penny. He'd worked too hard in his lifetime for that. Alyssa wasn't sure the plan would work, but they'd had lots of snacks and enjoyed themselves anyway.

As soon as they were done talking about that, the sisters relaxed. Alyssa's living room easily seated all five of them, and they had sausage rolls, chips and queso, and layered dip to occupy them. No one was complaining. Alyssa had enjoyed having someone to cook for. She didn't like cooking as a daily thing, but cooking for one event was always fun for her.

As always, the discussion went to the sisters' love lives.

Lauren looked at Alyssa first. "Are you still dating Tim?" She wrinkled her nose as she said Tim's name.

Alyssa sighed. "For today I am. I'm not sure how much longer it's going to last, to be honest with you. Things have been strange between us." She hated to admit she was ready to throw in the towel, but it was all she'd thought of for more than a week.

Taylor and Amanda exchanged looks.

"Is that good or bad?" Taylor asked.

"I'm not sure. On one hand, if I'm going to move on, I want to do it soon. On the other, I've put seven years into the relationship. It's time for him to fish or cut bait." Alyssa popped a cake ball into her mouth. She'd hit a bakery the night before to buy them, knowing her sisters would enjoy them but loving the excuse to eat badly herself. By the end of the weekend, they'd be trying to find the blood in her sugar stream.

Amanda smiled. "I think it's time to cut bait, whether it's his choice or yours. You don't need to be married to a man you're going to have to support for the rest of your life, you know."

"I do know." Alyssa shook her head, realizing no one in her life thought much of Tim. "I'm trying to decide what to do, and I'm really torn at the moment. I'll figure it out, though."

"I'm just glad you're finally considering ending it with him," Kayla said. "You're getting so thin. We're all worried about the way he has you eating and exercising. It's really good to see you eat people food instead of rabbit food today."

Alyssa frowned, realizing her sisters had all been worried about the way she ate. "Wanna know a secret?" she asked, leaning toward Kayla, who was sitting beside her on the couch.

"Sure. What's the secret?"

"I have emergency Junior Mints in my car. After a date, I usually scarf them down."

All the sisters laughed except Lauren. "I hate that you have to eat in secret, Alyssa. It's not healthy."

Alyssa was starting to feel ganged up on, and she shrugged. "We should play a game. It's been so long since we were all together for any period of time . . ." Hopefully her sisters would go for the idea, even though they'd know she was just trying to change the subject. They all loved playing games together.

"Do you still have Encore?" Amanda asked, naming a favorite game they all enjoyed. It had been out of print for years, and they all clung to their copy as best they could.

"I do! But I get to be on *your* team!" Alyssa knew that her sister had a memory for songs like no one else in the world, and she always wanted to be on her team when they played the singing game together.

The sisters quickly divided up into teams, and they played an entire game of Encore, which took them several hours. They ended up ordering a pizza and talking until after ten, when the sisters took turns leaving. There were hugs and promises to do it all again soon, but they all knew it wouldn't happen. It was a rare thing for them all to take time out of their busy lives to get together, but they were always glad when they did.

Alyssa had told the others to leave the mess, and she spent the hour after her last sister left running around picking up their trash from the day. She loaded the dishwasher, pleased that her snacks had gone over so well. The entire day had felt so good to her. She'd been busy laughing with people she loved.

When her doorbell rang, she glanced at the clock with a frown. One of her sisters must have forgotten something, and it must have been something important or they wouldn't have come back this late at night.

She opened the door wide without looking, surprised to see two police officers standing on her doorstep. Had they been so loud one of the neighbors called the police? She didn't think they had, but they must have been. It was the only reason she could think of that the police would be there.

The taller—and older—officer removed his hat. "Miss Romriell?"

"Yes, I'm Alyssa Romriell. How can I help you?" Now she was nervous. Had one of her sisters been in an accident on their way home from her house? There'd been no alcohol involved, but they had all left late. "Are my sisters all right?"

"May we come in?" The older officer was obviously taking the lead in the discussion.

Alyssa opened the door a little wider, leading them into the living room. "It's a bit of a mess. My sisters were here all day, and they just left. I'm cleaning up the last vestiges of the best sister party we've had in a very long time." She smiled at them nervously, wondering why she was talking so much.

"Please have a seat, Miss Romriell."

She knew it was bad, whatever they were there for. She sank onto the couch and watched as the two police officers sat in the overstuffed, flower-printed chairs perpendicular to the couch. "What is it?"

"I'm sorry to inform you that your parents were in a car accident a few hours ago. Your father died on impact. Your mother was rushed to the hospital, but she died shortly after the ambulance arrived. I'm very sorry for your loss."

Alyssa shook her head. He had to be confused. "No, that can't be. They were at the lake this weekend."

"Yes, the accident happened in Garden City."

"But my sisters and I figured out how to save the lake house. . . . We spent *hours!*"

The officer continued to watch her until it sank into her head. Her parents were just . . . gone. What did saving the lake house matter when her parents would never be in it with her again?

She let out a sob, stuffing her fist in her mouth to keep herself from wailing like a child. Gone. No more parents.

"I . . . what do I do?" She'd never dealt with this type of thing before, and she didn't feel equipped to do it.

The kind officer handed her a card with a phone number on it. "Call this number, and someone will help guide you through the next steps. Do you know if your parents had a will?"

She nodded. "Yes, of course."

"Contact the lawyer who represented them, and ask for a reading of the will. He'll help you with the process." It was advice that the man had obviously given many times.

The officer got to his feet, and the younger officer followed suit, speaking for the first time. "I'm very sorry for your loss."

"Thank you." The words were worthless. *Everything* was worthless now.

She saw the officers out and picked up her phone. It was late, but she needed to tell Tim first. He needed to be there for her. She tapped his number on the phone and closed her eyes.

He answered the phone, and she could hear loud music in the background. She wasn't surprised he was at a party. It was Saturday night, after all.

"Hullo?"

"Tim, it's Alyssa."

"What are you doing calling me so late?" he asked. He sounded annoyed with her.

She frowned. "I just wanted you to know that my parents died in a car wreck."

"Do your sisters know yet? I think you should be calling them, not me." Tim sounded as if he was talking to a small child, questioning her decision to call him and not someone more appropriate.

"Sure. I'll do that." She hung up and called her sisters. She'd go in age order again, because she was on autopilot now. She had to tell everyone who loved Mom and Dad. Everyone who would grieve with her over the death of her parents. Tim hadn't cared. Why should he? He obviously cared nothing for her any longer, if he ever had.

EIGHT

Alyssa's sisters came over the following morning. All of them looked as shell-shocked as she felt. She threw a huge pot of soup on the stove to feed them all, and they sat for a little while in the living room, just looking at each other. None of them could figure out what to say. Or do.

Alyssa swiped away a tear and started the conversation, needing the silence broken because they *had* to plan a funeral. How on earth were they supposed to plan something of that magnitude while they were still shell-shocked with grief? "While we're all here, we need to talk about the funeral. Mom and Dad chose the funeral home and their burial plot, but we need to decide who is speaking and what is happening. Anyone want to sing?" They all had sweet voices, so it was truly up to whoever thought they could sing at that time. "I'm thinking Wednesday for the service. Their lawyer is planning to come here on Thursday to talk about the will. We all need to be here for that."

Taylor swiped a tear from her eye. "I have the entire week off, so I'm good to help with whatever."

Lauren sniffled. "I could use help cleaning out their closets and such. I'm guessing we'll be getting the house ready to sell."

"Move in with me. You don't need those memories surrounding you. I think right now they'd hurt too much. We'll all go there Saturday and get it cleaned out . . . once we know what the lawyer has to say. You never know . . . maybe Mom and Dad were swimming in debt." Alyssa took her sister's hand in hers and gave it a squeeze. "I don't know that any of us need to be alone this week."

That got a smile from several of the sisters. "Slumber party at Alyssa's!" Lauren called, and there were a few chuckles.

"Remember that night when all the cousins went hunting for lightning bugs together?" Kayla asked. "We were up really late—which may have been eleven to my child mind—and we all slept in the living room telling stories of the Bear Lake ghost. I think we talked a little about the Bear Lake monster as well, but I can't quite remember for sure on that one. It was a favorite lake topic, though."

Amanda grinned. "We had the bugs in jars, and we kept them inside our sleeping bags. I tried to read by the light of the bugs, but they just weren't bright enough."

Alyssa shook her head. "We were all giggling half the night, and Dad finally came out and told us we needed to zip it and get some sleep."

Lauren frowned. "*Why* don't I remember this?" She obviously felt left out of the memory.

"Because you were about four," Alyssa told her sister. "One of the worst parts of being the youngest is not having all the fun memories the rest of us have." She nudged Lauren with her shoulder as they sat side-by-side on the couch. "What's your favorite memory of the lake?"

Lauren thought for a moment. "I remember being there one May, and we came up expecting to spend the week water skiing, but it snowed instead, so we made snowmen and built snow forts. And we did a little snowmobiling. It was amazing."

They all grinned at that.

"I remember that," Kayla said. "I remember a snowball fight, too, and I think it was Alyssa who threw a little too hard and a little too high . . ."

"And I broke the living room window, and Mom said no more snowballs, because if I was packing them that hard, I was going to give one of my sisters a concussion, and she wasn't making an emergency room trip because we didn't know how to behave when there was snow on the ground." Alyssa found herself laughing, and she surprised herself with it. Was it even okay to laugh right after your parents died? "Anyway, the funeral . . ."

Kayla raised her hand. "I'll sing. But I'm not singing 'Amazing Grace' or anything like that. I'm singing Colin Raye's 'Love Me.'" Her whole face crumpled as she named the song, and she buried her face in Lauren's shoulder, because Lauren was on the middle couch cushion. "I can't believe they're really dead."

Lauren wrapped her arm around Kayla, stroking her shoulder. "I can't either. This is crazy."

Amanda bowed her head for a moment, and when she lifted it, her eyes were bright with unshed tears. "What's your favorite memory of Dad?" she asked no one in particular.

Taylor was the first to respond. "Do you remember that first summer when Mom kept us all at the lake with her, and Dad would drive up on Thursday nights for a long weekend? Well, when he got there after being gone one weekend, he tried to teach me to ride one of the water scooters. I almost ran into a boat dock with it, and he was shaking his head at me. He told me that it would be Mom's job to teach me to drive because his nerves couldn't handle it." She shook her head. "I giggled and giggled, and then I told Mom, and Mom was laughing hysterically. When Dad came into the kitchen, she looked at him with a straight face and said, 'I think it's going to have to be your job to teach this girl to drive, Dwight. She just walked into a wall, and I can't be responsible for that.' Dad's face went pure white, but he nodded. I don't think he ever realized she was just having fun with him."

The sisters laughed, even as they struggled through their tears.

"I can just see it," Kayla said. "Dad would never ask Mom to do something he didn't think he could do himself."

"Do you remember the time Mom backed into the mailbox at the lake house, and she paid a neighbor to fix the mailbox, but she kept the van in the garage all weekend so Dad wouldn't see it? She got it taken care of while he was at work the next week. We were all sworn to secrecy, and I remember giggling about it with Hannah." Alyssa grinned. "Mom always said she never kept secrets from Dad, but I don't know if he ever found out about that fender bender."

"Probably not." Amanda scooted to the floor and hugged her knees to her, reminding Alyssa of the way she'd sat when they were small.

"So, Kayla's singing. Does anyone feel up to the eulogy?" Alyssa asked. She knew they had to get this planned, whether they wanted to or not. The funeral preparations were the main priority for the day. That and grieving.

Lauren sniffed once more. "I didn't take all those public speaking classes for nothing. I'll do it."

Alyssa typed the note into her phone with her thumbs. "I want to tell people not to send flowers. They should donate the money instead. But to what?" She had no desire to deal with a million flowers. They would just remind her that their parents were gone.

"Battered women," Amanda said, avoiding Alyssa's eyes. "I think there should be a lot more education on just what kind of behavior qualifies as abuse. Some of the smartest women I know have stayed in abusive relationships for years, feeling like they deserved what they got."

"I can agree with that." Though Alyssa knew her sister was talking about her, she believed in the cause. The others all agreed, and she made a note. "I'm supposed to have a conference call this evening with the funeral home director, so I'd like all the little details lined up." She glanced up at her sisters. "Do we want a meal provided? I know it's customary, but I'd rather it just be the five of us grieving together and not a bunch of people we don't know."

Taylor tilted her head to one side. "I would rather it just be us as well. We'll go to Dad's favorite restaurant, and we can just be together with no one patting us and telling us how sorry they are for our loss."

"I think that's a brilliant idea," Amanda said. "We'll just meet up at the Longhorn in Ogden and hope we can get Brandi for our waitress. Dad liked her best."

"Oh, Dad just liked to eat," Kayla said. "Remember that time he tried to make ribs on the grill, and they were burnt? He'd been thinking about those ribs all day, so he took us all the way to North Salt Lake just so he could eat ribs. We were all asleep before we got back to the lake house."

Alyssa frowned. "What are we going to do with the lake house? None of us wanted it sold, and I would bet Mom and Dad left it to all of us together."

"And the house in Kaysville," Lauren added. "That's two houses. And Mom's car is paid for."

"I think you get the car," Taylor said to Lauren. "You're the only one of us without a new car. Yours is a demolition derby reject."

"Hey! Be nice to Galahad."

"That old boat does *not* deserve to be called Galahad," Amanda said. "He should be called rust bucket or something."

Lauren crossed her arms over her chest as if she was angry. "I don't like you guys dissing my car, but you're right. I do need a new one. If only for job searches. Maybe I'll start searching for jobs at the lake."

"I think we should Airbnb the lake house," Alyssa said softly. "We all need to think about exactly what we want, and we can talk after Mr. Kunz leaves on Thursday. We'll have a better idea of what we need to be discussing then."

"Do we need to disclose the secret passages on Airbnb?" Taylor asked, her eyes full of memories. "Remember how none of the cousins knew about the secret passages and they just thought we were the best hide and seekers ever? I loved being able to go through the bookcase in the downstairs living room and pop up into the family room upstairs, and from there we could go anywhere. And they thought they were so smart guarding the stairs. Especially Ben. He was such a dork about it."

Ben was their cousin, and he was Alyssa's age. He'd thought he was so smart, but he'd never figured out any of the passages.

"And all of the passages between the bedrooms upstairs? I always giggled when we played Clue because of those secret passages. I was sure he was going to figure it out, but he never did." Amanda shook her head. "It's hard to believe he's a doctor now when he was so *dense* as a kid."

Kayla looked far away. "My favorite part of being at the lake was always helping Mom with the flowers . . ."

"You complained about it whenever it was your turn!" Alyssa said with a frown.

"I know I did, but looking back at the long talks we each got to have with Mom as we helped, I realize it was the highlight of my summers. We each put in an hour of work every day, and my favorite was when I got to sit with Mom, surrounded by the beauty she always made sure enveloped the lake house, and she would talk to me about anything that was on my mind. Sometimes I just wanted to talk about my dreams of building a treehouse in the big oak tree in the back . . ."

Lauren sighed. "I loved that treehouse. It had *eight floors*."

"It did!" Kayla grinned. "I could build even then. Dad always called me his favorite son."

"Is the treehouse even still there?" Alyssa asked. "It's been so long since I've been to the lake . . ."

"It is," Lauren said. "I was there a few years ago. It's looking a little dilapidated, but I think with a fresh coat of paint and a hammer and nails used by someone who knew how to use them, it would be perfect again."

Kayla smiled. "I'll make sure to take some the next time I go."

Alyssa thought she looked excited at the prospect of working on her first real building project as an adult.

As the day wore on, they made the rest of the arrangements for the funeral, but more importantly, they shared memories of their parents at their favorite place in the entire world.

The later it got, the more the sisters realized they didn't want to split up. They had all made sure they had off until the following Monday, and they planned to take the time to just be together and grieve.

"Do you still have real-sized clothes?" Amanda finally asked Alyssa. "You know, like you wore BT?"

Alyssa started to ask what BT meant, but she realized it meant Before Tim. Her sisters had always measured her life before and after he'd come into her life. "I do. In one of the spare rooms. And I have a washer and dryer. And extra toothbrushes and toothpaste, and so much room. Please stay." They all knew she didn't want to be alone, but none of them blamed her. They didn't want to be alone either. No, it was a week for the sisters to stay together.

"I get the green room," Amanda said, getting to her feet and stretching. "I'm going to find nightgowns for all of us, and we'll throw the clothes we're wearing into the washer. It won't hurt any of us to wear them two nights in a row."

Together, they went about their pre-bedtime routines, and they found clothes that fit. They would stay together as long as they could get away with it, because only together could they face the overwhelming grief of losing two of the greatest people they'd ever known. Dwight and Elizabeth Romriell.

NINE

THE DAY of the funeral was long and arduous, and the sisters were glad they'd made the decision to have a joint funeral for their beloved parents. They couldn't go through this twice in such a short period of time. Kayla sang, and there wasn't a dry eye in the place. Lauren spoke, her voice strong and steady, despite the tears running down her face.

All five sisters stood in a line as people left the funeral home where the service had been held.

"Your father saved me from years of migraine pain," one woman stopped to say. Alyssa didn't recognize her, and she doubted her sisters did either, but they heard stories like that over and over as people walked past them, shaking their hands or embracing them, depending on how well they knew them.

The funeral home was filled completely, with people standing at the back to pay their respects.

It took more than an hour for the five sisters to accept condolences from everyone in the group, and then they drove to the cemetery, where a brief prayer was spoken by the pastor of the church they'd all grown up attending. They had chosen a headstone that was for both parents, because they all felt as if their parents wouldn't want to be separated—even in death.

As soon as they had each sprinkled dirt on the caskets, Alyssa led the others to their cars, which had been first in line between the funeral home and the cemetery, and then they followed their plans exactly.

They all drove back to Alyssa's house, where they were staying for the week. Everyone had collected their clothes, and they took Alyssa's car to Longhorn. When they walked in, they requested Brandi. She was on her way out the door, but she saw the sisters and said, "They're mine. I'll stay for them."

After they'd been seated, Brandi came over to check on the sisters, showing them pictures from the cruise she'd taken recently with her daughters. "What brings you girls in today? Your dad isn't here. Are you allowed to come without him?" The words were said jokingly, but only Lauren—who seemed to have a gift for speaking through pain—was able to answer.

"Mom and Dad were killed in a car accident on Saturday night. We're here to commemorate their lives, rather than eating with a bunch of strangers who tell us how sorry they are." Lauren had tears in her eyes, and Brandi gasped, sinking down into a seat at the table with them.

"I'm so sorry. I had no idea." Brandi reached for the hand of the sister closest to her, Taylor, as she sat, absolutely stunned at the news. "I can't believe it."

Alyssa nodded. "Trust me. We understand. It's all we've been able to say since we got the news. Funeral was today, and reading of the will is tomorrow."

"I don't even know what to say. I loved your parents. You all know that. I'll be praying for peace for all of you as you go through this." Brandi shook her head. "Who gets the job of sorting out the estate?"

"Probably Alyssa," Lauren said. "She's oldest and good at stuff like that. We won't know for sure until we've talked to the lawyer, though."

Brandi pulled out a pad. "What drinks do you want? Let me at least feed you since I can't take your pain away."

They all ordered their drinks and talked softly as Brandi hurried away to get them.

"Even waiters and waitresses loved Mom and Dad. What are we going to do without them?" Kayla asked, her eyes bleak.

Alyssa shook her head at her sister. "That's not why we're here. We went to the funeral to mourn and to grieve. We're here to have a celebration of their lives as only the people who loved them best are able to have."

Brandi came with the drinks, catching the last thing Alyssa had said. She had tears in her eyes. "I'll start off your celebration by telling you my favorite thing about each of your parents. Dwight was always so giving and generous. Any time he saw a group of police officers, he'd make sure to pay their bill. Same with any of the armed forces. He was kind. One of the busboys spilled an entire plate of food on him, and he just cleaned it off, didn't get angry, and didn't ask for any money off his check.

"Elizabeth was so gentle, and she loved you girls more than anything else on this earth. She would talk about each of you. When Lauren graduated from college, she brought me pictures of her in her cap and gown and all five of you together. She called you her precious girls. Everyone in this place knew who they were, and they were loved by everyone whose lives they touched."

All five sisters had tears in their eyes at the beautiful, unexpected tribute.

"Thank you," Kayla said. "We needed to hear how other people saw them today."

Brandi brushed away her own tears. "I'll be back in a few minutes to get your order, but there's no hurry. I'm here as long as you girls are." She hurried away from them, going back into the kitchen. She obviously needed to compose herself as well.

Alyssa smiled. "Let's figure out what we want to eat so we don't keep Brandi forever, and then we'll go around the table. First everyone can say what they thought was Dad's best quality. And then we'll do it all again for Mom. We're celebrating the wonderful people who gave birth to us today. We can grieve more tomorrow, but *today* is for loving them."

It was an hour and a half and much laughter and tears later when they left the restaurant. They'd had six different people who worked for the place come to the table and offer their condolences, all of them mentioning what they would miss most about their parents.

On the drive back to Alyssa's house, they stopped by the grocery store and bought all of the comfort food they could find. They needed to grieve, and they would do it together, the same way they'd done so many other things together. As a family.

After the groceries were put away, they all changed into comfortable clothes. No more black dresses for them. No, they were going to stay together and handle things the best way they knew how. It was the only answer.

TEN

On Thursday, Mr. Kunz, their father's long-time friend and attorney, was at Alyssa's house to read the will. He counted heads to make sure all the sisters were there before beginning.

"I'm not going to read it word for word, because there's no need for that. The will is simply a practical list of who gets what. I'm sure all of you will appreciate that." He glanced down at the document in his hand. "Lauren, you get your mother's Subaru Forester. They wanted you to have something safe to drive and not 'that old rattletrap.'"

Lauren smiled slightly. "I can just hear Dad saying that, too. He kept trying to buy me a car, but I didn't want to take charity."

"Well, you have no choice now." Mr. Kunz looked back at the will. "Alyssa, your parents would like you to deal with the sale of their home, and whatever money comes from it needs to be split five ways for all of you to share."

Alyssa nodded. "I expected that." It would keep her busy as well. It was good that it had been her assignment, and the sisters would work together to get everything cleaned out and sold.

He went on to list many of the things their parents had accumulated over the years. Alyssa was to get their mother's china collection, and Taylor was to receive their bedroom suite, which she had always admired.

Each daughter received something that she considered special, but they all waited with bated breath to hear what was said about the lake house.

"Now, for the house at Bear Lake." He smiled as he watched each sister lean forward. "Your father was very specific about that house. He wants all of you to own it together, or he wants it sold and the money split evenly among you. I got the impression he wanted you to share it."

The sisters all exchanged glances. It was what they wanted.o

The last thing Mr. Kunz said surprised all of them. "I'm going to read this last line to you, and then I'll be done. 'To my daughter Alyssa's best friend, Hannah Baldwin, I leave the sum of two hundred thousand dollars. My daughters won't miss it, and that girl has worked harder than anyone should have to earning money for her bookstore. Hannah, you've always been a sixth daughter to me, and know that we loved you with all our hearts. Use the money wisely.' The rest of the assets your parents had will be liquidated and split evenly among you. Are there any questions?"

The sisters exchanged looks. "Who will see to the selling off of the assets?" Alyssa asked. She knew she was selling the house in town, but she wasn't sure if she was supposed to be in charge of that as well.

"I was asked to do that, and I'll retain a small fee for my services. Your father and I worked all that out years ago."

Alyssa got to her feet and shook hands with Mr. Kunz. "Thank you so much for your time."

"Your father was a wonderful man, and he will be missed by so many."

Alyssa walked him to the door after accepting a copy of the will.

She was actually excited to call Hannah and let her know about the money which had been left to her. She knew her friend would be ecstatic. Well, she'd be ecstatic with a portion of the news she had to share.

Walking back to the couch, she sat down between Taylor and Kayla. "Does anyone mind if I call Hannah and let her know what was decided? And then we'll discuss the lake house."

Taylor had a half smile on her face. "I have some ideas for the lake house. I just hope everyone will hear me out before they start arguing."

"That sounds ominous," Amanda said. "You worry me, Taylor."

Alyssa smiled as she left the room and walked down the hallway and into her bedroom. The room was decorated in lilac and white. It was definitely a female room. Her bed was king size, and she had a row of shelves above her head. She and Amanda had shopped for the furniture together, and Amanda had taken it from there. Sitting on her bed, Alyssa dialed her friend's number. Hannah came on the phone right away.

"You caught me between jobs. What's up, buttercup?" The happiness in Hannah's voice to hear from her struck Alyssa as odd until she remembered that her friend hadn't heard the news yet.

"So . . . I have bad news and good news. If you have ten minutes to pull over, it might be best." Alyssa didn't want to risk another accident by telling her friend while she was driving. Hannah had always been close to Alyssa's parents.

"I have time. Just give me a second. I'll pull into a gas station." There was a moment, and then Hannah said, "But you're scaring me making me pull over. I've done it."

"Mom and Dad were killed in a car wreck on Saturday night." Alyssa couldn't soften the truth. She'd given the news one too many times that week, and she just didn't have it in her to beat around the bush about it.

"What? No!" Hannah sounded truly distraught. "How can there be good news after that?"

"Well, the will was read today, and my parents left you two hundred grand to go toward your bookstore. They think it's time you started building it and stopped working so many jobs."

Hannah said nothing for a moment, and Alyssa waited.

"Hannah?"

"I don't even know what to say. I'm shocked and broken about your parents, but that kind of money? You and your sisters should split that between you. I wasn't their child to leave anything to."

Alyssa had expected that answer, but she wasn't accepting it. "No. Dad was very specific that he wanted you to have it and what he wanted you to use it for. Besides, he said you were his sixth daughter and he'd always thought of you that way. They left us plenty. I promise."

"I'm sure. Wow. I don't even know what to say. I'm so sorry they died, Lyss. I can't imagine what you must be feeling."

Hannah's soft voice commiserating with her had the tears flowing for Alyssa again. "I've had several days to process it, and my sisters and I have been together almost constantly, working through our feelings about it." Alyssa didn't say she was fine, because she was far from fine, but she was doing better than she had been a few days before.

"I wish I could hug you, but that's not happening from this distance. You girls need to come to the lake soon and see me."

"You know? I think that's going to happen. We've talked about happy memories from the lake house all week. I think we need to go there and grieve together. Or maybe party together. We seem to be alternating between the two."

Hannah laughed softly. "I'm not surprised. You and your sisters have always been a bit odd."

"Oh, please. Have you looked in a mirror lately?" Alyssa felt a lot better now that she'd told Hannah. When she'd called Tim, she just needed to share with someone who wouldn't grieve as much as she had. He'd refused to allow that, though.

"Well, I'm going to let you go and head to Coopers. I have a full night ahead of me."

"Not for much longer," Alyssa said, relieved that her father had included her friend in his generosity. She knew Hannah would make good use of the money.

Alyssa walked back into the living room, joining her sisters, who were discussing food.

"I just want to order another pizza," Lauren said. "None of us feel like cooking. Or we could do something from grub hub. Or order something else. I just don't want to cook."

Alyssa took a spot on the floor. "I'm up for whatever. Pizza sounds pretty good, actually." Her years of pizza deprivation were catching up with her, and she refused to suffer through any more of it. Pizza was the answer.

They talked and discussed what they wanted, and Taylor put in an order for two large pizzas. As soon as she was finished, she folded her hands on her lap, seeming nervous. "I have an idea about the lake house."

"What's the idea?" Alyssa felt a bit skeptical. Her sister looked like she was up to something.

It didn't take long before every sister was looking at Taylor, waiting to hear her idea.

"Let's turn it into a bed and breakfast. We can all move to the lake. There's enough room for all five of us and still have seven guestrooms to rent out. More if we're willing to double up. I can run the place. We can do a total remodel and hire someone to work with Kayla on it. I think we all need a fresh start, and this week has showed me that we need each other. A lot."

Alyssa frowned. "I'm not licensed in Idaho." She couldn't give up her job to help run a B&B. Besides, it shouldn't take all five of them to run it.

"How hard would it be to get licensed there? You know your stuff. Shouldn't you just have to take a test or something?"

"Probably. But what about Tim?" Alyssa knew her sisters didn't like him, but all she could think about were the seven years they had together. Why would she give up seven years now?

"Dump the jerk. I want to use worse language, but I'm a lady," Lauren said, folding her hands demurely on her lap.

They all laughed at that.

"I don't know if I'm ready," Alyssa said honestly.

Amanda frowned at Alyssa. "How long has it been since the two of you went out together when he didn't need money? How long since he paid for a meal?"

"I—" Alyssa had no answers. She truly couldn't remember.

"How long since you went out with him and he didn't make you feel like you were lacking?" Kayla asked. "You're a beautiful woman who has gotten much too thin thanks to his machinations. You need to be taking care of yourself, not worrying about him."

Listening to her sisters, Alyssa realized that they were right. He had messed with her head for altogether too long. "All right. I'm in."

"You are?" Taylor asked, looking shocked. "I thought you would be the hardest to convince."

They went around the room, and each sister agreed to do it.

"I like the idea of working together," Amanda said. "I want to turn the rooms into themed rooms. Famous romantic couples or something. I'll think on it. I seriously can't wait to get started. I have two more jobs I've agreed to do here, and I'll be ready to go. Well, and Alyssa will have to sell my house."

Alyssa laughed. "I have a feeling I'll be selling lots of houses. Starting with my own."

Slowly their plans started to take shape. When the doorbell rang, Alyssa jumped up to get the pizza. She opened the door and was surprised to see Tim. "What are you doing here?" she asked. She could almost feel her sisters straining to listen to the conversation. He only stopped by when he wanted something. Hopefully he hadn't put it together that her parents were dead and she was due to inherit.

Tim frowned. "Can't a boyfriend go to see his girlfriend?"

She shook her head. "No, because you're not my boyfriend anymore. You wouldn't even talk to me when I found out my parents had just died. What kind of boyfriend would do that? I'm afraid I'm completely done with you." Telling him was easier than she'd thought it would be, and it felt so freeing.

"You can't mean that! We've dated for years."

"Yes, we have, and you have ruined my life in a lot of different ways. Not only am I breaking things off with you, I'm moving to Idaho, and I don't plan to see you again." She started to close the door, but he put his foot in the way.

"Wait . . . I know you're done with me, and I guess I can understand that, but can't we at least stay friends?"

"No, I don't think we can. Friends accept each other for who they are. They don't expect them to make changes to be seen with them." Alyssa knew she wouldn't have had the courage to say everything if her sisters hadn't been sitting right there, listening to her. But they gave her the strength she needed.

"Well, if we can't be friends, can I at least get one last loan? I need a thousand dollars. My car is about to be repossessed."

Alyssa was just about to say no when she felt someone walk up behind her and close the door. Tim's foot was still in the door, and he yelled 'ouch!' as he got out of the way. She turned to see Taylor standing behind her. Until that moment, Alyssa hadn't realized she was shaking.

Taylor hugged her. "It's over. Tim's gone, and you don't ever have to see him again."

Taking a deep breath, Alyssa nodded, feeling very fragile for a moment. "Thank you."

"Go sit, and I'll get the pizza when it comes." Taylor pushed her toward the living room. "Lauren, get some plates and napkins. Amanda, you're on drinks. We're having an 'Alyssa finally dumped Tim' party, and we're going to plan our bed and breakfast. If we hurry, we might be able to have it open by June first for tourist season. It's going to be a lot of work, but I think we can do it."

Alyssa moved to sit in one of her chairs, and she thought about it. She could see how they could make it work. It wouldn't be easy, but with five of them working together, anything was possible.

At least for a while, they'd all be sharing a house. That worried her, remembering some of their early fights, but most of them had means to stay elsewhere if necessary. They'd make it work.

ELEVEN

THE NEXT FEW weeks were filled with activity for Alyssa. She and her sisters went through their parents' house and organized everything. They donated many items of clothing and divided treasures up between them.

Some of the furniture they decided they wanted to keep for the lake house, and others they sold in an estate sale. It felt to Alyssa that every minute she wasn't working, she was doing something to get ready for the move, including selling her parents' house, her own, Taylor's, and Amanda's.

Kayla was a house flipper, so she lived in whatever property she was fixing up at any given time. She wouldn't be quite done when the other sisters were, so she would stay behind and finish the house before she put it up for sale.

They had a target move date of April fifteenth, which gave them just a month after the funeral to get everything ready.

Alyssa stopped working out with Barbie, no longer needing the validation that came from working out with her. She was happy to never have to see the woman again. She was sure she would keep up some form of exercise, but torturing herself no longer needed to be on the agenda.

On the day before the sale closed on her parents' house in Kaysville, the five of them went there and made sure it was cleaned and ready to go. They could have hired someone to do it—and even discussed that option—but they decided they wanted to do it together.

They'd grown up in that house, and selling it was hard for all of them. Splitting the house up into sections, each sister took a section, and they worked side-by-side, doing the type of cleaning their mother had taught them to do as children.

When they finished, Lauren hurried out to her car and brought in plates and napkins. "We're having one more pizza party in the middle of the living room floor. I have a picnic blanket in my old room."

Kayla went to get the blanket, and they spread it out while they waited for the pizza to arrive.

"I can't believe how good you look," she said to Alyssa as they all sat down for their feast.

Alyssa smiled. She'd put on five pounds, and when she looked in a mirror, she could see that her cheeks were rounder and her face looked softer. "I still work out, but I'm not working myself into a frenzy. And I'm eating like a normal person again. No more twigs."

They all laughed at that. "You really do look so much better than you did. I think Tim would have made you starve yourself, and he still would have thought you were too heavy to be seen with him." Amanda shook her head. "But look at you now! As beautiful as ever."

Alyssa blushed and changed the subject. "So, this house closes tomorrow. Amanda's house closes Tuesday, and Taylor's on Wednesday." There had been so much packing done in the past month across different homes that they all felt a little achy all the time. There wouldn't be as much room as they would need at the lake house, so the sisters rented out a large storage unit, and all of their things were there, with boxes clearly labeled so they wouldn't forget whose box was whose.

"And when does yours close again?" Taylor asked Alyssa. "I know you have to love us to let all of us move in with you this week."

"I love you a lot until the novelty of feeling like sisters again wears off. I'm sure we'll be at each other's throats in a month like we were when we were little girls." Alyssa hoped she was wrong as she picked up a slice of pizza.

The house looked so different than they were used to. It was now completely devoid of furniture, and the curtains were even taken down. It was strange to think it would be their last time in that house. Alyssa had her first kiss on the front porch, with her little sisters peeking out the window at her.

"I'd say I don't see that happening," Taylor said, "but I sure remember how bossy you can get." They'd all agreed that Taylor would need to be in charge of the bed and breakfast. She had the training, after all.

"I'm the oldest. I'm supposed to be bossy," Alyssa said, grinning at her. "I was just thinking that my first kiss was on that doorstep. All of us took our first steps in this house. Why don't we have the emotional attachment to this place that we have to the lake house?"

"I think it's because this was the place we did our homework. Where we had to go to school every day. Where we did our chores. The lake house was the fun place, where we all wanted to be all the time," Amanda said. She'd obviously already given the subject some thought.

"Maybe," Taylor said, shrugging. "I'm not sure why it is, but the lake house has a lot more meaning for me as well."

"So, my house sells on Monday," Alyssa said. "I figure Monday afternoon, we all get in our cars and drive up to the lake. The mover will be at my place at noon Monday, and they're going to pack it all up. We'll caravan." They couldn't drive together, because they all would want their cars when they got up to the lake. Unlike Salt Lake City, there was no public transportation at the lake.

They had made a few trips up with boxes and put them into the garage, but none of the sisters had actually stayed at the lake house since the decision had been made. They planned to modernize the kitchen and redo some of the bathrooms. The house was already perfect for what they were planning, though. There were twelve bedrooms, and even if they each lived there—which they would initially, but probably not forever—there would still be seven rooms for guests.

The house had been built with the entire extended family in mind. Aunts, uncles, and cousins had piled into the house with them for two weeks every summer, which was why they had such good memories. There were three garages with two bays each, and they had already had a small parking lot poured off to one side of the house. That had been one of the toughest decisions they'd made, because their mother would have been mortified to know they had taken away some of her garden space. Still, it was for the best.

"I'm excited to sleep at the lake house on Monday night," Lauren said. "I feel like it's been forever since we all went up there as a family. I almost asked for that for my graduation from Utah State in December, but I didn't want it to be a hardship for all of you, and driving there in the snow is always a hardship."

"I have news for you, Lauren," Alyssa said. "It's still snowing up there now. We're going to have snow for a while yet, and we're going to be living there in the winters. Snow will happen, just like it happens here."

"But we're getting snowmobiles," Lauren said. "I think we should have them for people to rent. We might as well make the money rather than letting someone else have their business."

"True," Taylor said. "I have lots of ideas for running the place. I'm so excited to have a bed and breakfast where all of the owners are related to me and I have a say in renovations. This is a dream come true for me."

Alyssa looked at her sister with a smile. It was nice to be able to help her with her dream. She herself would still be selling real estate, but she would be doing it in a slower-paced world. And truly, she couldn't wait to see what came of Hannah's bookstore. Her friend had already quit working at the grocery store, and she was no longer cleaning on the weekends. She wasn't sure if she'd broken ground yet, but she knew it would be happening soon.

The last meal at the house where they'd grown up turned into another kind of celebration for all of them. A celebration of their lives changing and them giving up all of their old dreams to make new ones.

They all went their separate ways after supper, except for Lauren, who went home with Alyssa. As they got into Lauren's vehicle, Alyssa sank back into the seat.

"I think it's best you haven't found a job yet," Alyssa said. "You'll be able to do some of the work at the B&B." Alyssa knew she herself wouldn't be working there, and neither would Kayla. Taylor would be there full time, and they were thinking that Lauren would as well. Amanda would work there long enough to get the B&B ready to open, but then she'd be looking for other work as well.

"Probably. I can clean rooms, and maybe I can figure out how to make breakfast interesting. I've always enjoyed cooking, and with my liberal arts degree, I have the ability to read cookbooks."

Alyssa laughed. "You have the ability to do a whole lot more than read cookbooks."

"I know. But if I can't make a joke out of my liberal arts degree, then who can?" Lauren drove calmly through the city. "Are you worried about leaving your job?"

"Not at all. I still have closings scheduled for another month out, so I'll have income coming in. Not that any of us really need immediate income, but it's nice to not feel like a wastrel. I hate the idea of having to study for tests all over again, but I'll do it because I love what I do. I guess I could sell in Garden City, because I'm already licensed in Utah, but I like the idea of being able to work in the entire area. All of Bear Lake."

"Makes sense to me." Lauren shook her head. "I can't believe we've gotten so much done in just a month. I guess it just goes to show that the five of us together can do absolutely anything we set our minds to."

Alyssa smiled at that. "We can."

When Lauren pulled into the driveway in front of Alyssa's house, she spotted Tim's car, and she groaned. "Tim's here."

Alyssa sighed. "I wonder what he wants. I haven't seen anything of him since the day the will was read."

"Do you want me to get rid of him?" Lauren asked. "I know karate, kung fu, and several other Japanese words!"

Laughing, Alyssa shook her head. "I'll deal with him."

"I'm not leaving you alone with that jerk," Lauren said, getting out and walking over to Tim with her sister.

"What can I do for you, Tim?" Alyssa asked, keeping her voice cordial.

"I miss you. What would it take for you to take me back?" He wasted no time getting to the point.

"I'm afraid that ship has sailed. There's no way I'm taking you back. I'm moving next week, and I'm ready to start fresh." Alyssa didn't bother to soften her words with him.

Tim narrowed his eyes. "Is there a man there? Are you dating someone already?"

Alyssa shook her head. "Of course not. I'm opening a bed and breakfast with my sisters, and I'm going to be happy."

"You are, are you?" he asked.

"Yes, I am. And nothing you can say or do is going to stop me."

Tim frowned at her. "I can't believe you're treating me this badly."

Lauren could no longer hold her tongue. "She's treating *you* badly? You have *got* to be kidding me! You've mentally abused her for years, and you're going to get off her property, or I'm calling the cops." She grabbed her sister's upper arm and pulled her toward the door. "And no, you can't have more money!"

Lauren unlocked the door and walked in with her sister, slamming it behind her. "That man has some nerve. I hope I never lay eyes on him again."

"You and me both." Alyssa was proud of herself, though. She'd been strong and clear she wasn't getting back with him, and she hadn't even wanted to. It was a huge step in the right direction.

TWELVE

Alyssa closed on her house as soon as the title company opened on Monday morning. She'd had her house for several years, but she certainly wasn't as tied to it as she was to the lake house. Still, she was sad to let it go but excited at the same time. She was getting a new start with the people she loved more than anything. It was time for sister power.

She'd signed the last document, assisted by Jennifer Whitcomb, a woman she'd worked with the entire time she'd been a real estate agent. They were both well aware this was their last closing together, and they were emotional. When she signed in the last space, she lifted her hand and rubbed her wrist.

"Wow. I can't believe I make people sign their name that many times on a regular basis," Alyssa joked.

"Well, you're really going to be missed around here." Jennifer turned and grabbed a big basket filled with healthy snacks. "We put this together for you to wish you safe travels and a wonderful new life with your sisters."

Alyssa hugged the girl, and she found herself hugging three more people on her way out. "Thanks, everyone, for the sweet gift. I'm going to miss all of you."

She left amidst choruses of goodbye. She knew it wouldn't be the last time she saw them all, but it would certainly not be a weekly thing any longer. Keeping her real estate license in Utah was part of her plan. If she ever needed to come back, she could, though she couldn't imagine that happening at the moment.

She drove home, knowing her sisters were waiting for her. All of their homes had been closed on, and all of them except Kayla planned to make the drive up to Bear Lake together. Kayla had a month of work to do at the house, and she would join them in Bear Lake as soon as it was finished.

At Alyssa's house, there was already a moving truck, and things were being loaded into it. Lauren had taken the lead, telling the movers which things to load in first because they were going into storage.

Alyssa parked at the curb, watching her baby sister bossing around the moving men for a little while, and then she got out of the car. She looked lovingly at the house. It had been her first big purchase after completing her training to be a real estate agent, and she had been so proud of it. She'd moved from her parents' home into this one, and it felt . . . strange to be leaving it behind. She knew she was being overly sentimental, but she couldn't help it.

She walked over to Lauren, smiling at her kid sister. "Thanks for being the bossy little thing you are."

Lauren grinned. "I'm happy to be bossy if it helps."

"I'm going to go in and start vacuuming the rooms they've finished." Alyssa wasn't looking forward to doing a good cleaning of the house, but it was required.

"Taylor's already doing that."

"Okay, then I'll go in and scrub out the oven and fridge."

Lauren shook her head. "I did that as soon as you left this morning."

"Bathrooms? Kitchen floor?"

"All done. We split the work between us, because you let us all stay here while we were getting ready to start our new adventure." Lauren put her arm around Alyssa. "Just sit back and enjoy the show."

"The show?" Alyssa asked.

"Well, the youngest guy is pretty darn cute. I just wish it was hot enough that he had to take his shirt off . . ."

Alyssa laughed. "Maybe you should spill something on him." She walked into the now mostly empty house and went from room to room, loving the colors she'd painted different things. Her curtains had been removed, and all of her special little touches were gone. Packed away and sent to storage. Only the things she would truly *need* were going to the new house. For a moment, she felt her heart beat faster as she wondered how she was going to manage, but she knew she could. She'd have her sisters at her sides.

As soon as the movers had the truck all packed up, Alyssa, Lauren, Amanda, and Taylor walked through every room in the house, making sure nothing important had been left behind. So many memories had been made in the house, and they were leaving that, too.

Alyssa felt a bit panicked that they were leaving everything they knew behind to start this new adventure, but when she looked at her sisters' faces, she knew they were doing the right thing. They had to be.

They each had a suitcase with several days' worth of clothes and toiletries in their cars, and they were as ready as they were going to get.

"All right. Let's get this show on the road. I do want to stop in Logan for supplies, because they'll be so much cheaper than in Bear Lake. I'm sure we'll do most of our shopping locally, but this one last time, Logan will work." Alyssa led the way out of the house, locking her door for the very last time. A lovely couple with three children was moving in, and they would make their own memories there.

She swiped away a tear as she went to her car. "Remember, cellphones on at all times. If someone needs to stop, honk, and we'll all stop." She wished they could ride together, but they would all need cars at their new home. "See you all in Logan." Logan was the halfway point between Salt Lake City and Bear Lake. They would stop there for some food, fuel, and groceries.

Alyssa led the way, pulling away from the curb and waiting as each of her sisters fell into line behind her. She knew this was the right thing, but it still broke her heart to do it.

An hour and a half later, Alyssa pulled into Olive Garden in Logan, and all the other sisters followed suit. She got out of the car to stretch her legs, wishing she hadn't done so much packing leading up to the move. She was sore, and she was going to be for a few days.

The four of them walked into the restaurant and were seated at the back. "I'm glad we decided on a late lunch. I don't want to be overrun with college kids," Lauren said, shaking her head.

Logan was a college town, but given the fact that Lauren was a recent grad, the other three found her statement very funny.

Amanda was the one who pointed out what she'd said, though. "You act like college students are such a pain. You know you were one just a few months ago, right?"

"I feel like I acted more mature than college students do today."

Alyssa shook her head. "I love you, but . . . you're crazy."

The waitress stopped there then, a big grin on her face. She'd obviously heard what Alyssa said. "Sisters, right?"

All four siblings nodded.

"Sure are," Taylor said. She looked at the others. "Are we all done deciding what we want?" She was obsessed with keeping them on schedule. There was so much to be done before they could open the B&B.

Every one of them nodded. "All right. Give me your drink orders first, and then I'll take the food orders."

An hour later, they were back on the road, but only for a short distance, heading to Walmart next.

"I hate Walmart," Lauren said, frowning. "Do we *have* to shop here?"

"Yes," Alyssa responded. "And everyone is supposed to hate Walmart. It's a requirement for living in the United States. But they always have the best prices, and that's what we need."

"Ugh."

By the time they reached Bear Lake, they were all exhausted. Alyssa pulled into the driveway of the house where they'd spent so much time, and she felt her excitement build. She was finally home.

Getting out, each sister carried in her personal things, and Alyssa took the key and unlocked the door. The house was a little messy.

"It never occurred to me that Mom and Dad were actually *staying* here when they died." She walked through the house, putting a couple of glasses into the dishwasher, picking up her mother's reading glasses. So many little things that reminded them of what they'd lost.

When she reached the master bedroom, Alyssa was surprised to see that the bed wasn't made. Her mother had always harped on them about keeping their beds made, and when no one was looking, she didn't make her own. She wished her mother was there so she could tease her—and for so many other reasons.

"Are you taking the master?" Taylor asked her from behind.

"I don't care. Does it matter?" Alyssa asked. She knew that her sisters considered it hers by right because she was the oldest.

Taylor shrugged. "Because there's a cubby hole where a desk can be put, I was kind of hoping you wouldn't mind if I took it. I'll be the one running the place, and having this room would make things just a bit easier for me."

Alyssa nodded. "I think things would be easier for *me* if you took the room. I'll go to the one next door."

The house was just as they all remembered. There was a living room on the first floor and a family room on the second. Each story had six bedrooms. There were seven bathrooms on each floor. Above the kitchen was a huge room that they'd used as a play room over the years. It was a room that really wasn't necessarily meant to be anything, but there had been more slumber parties on that floor that any of the girls could remember. It hadn't really been updated since the nineties, so many things were out of date. Alyssa could see there was a lot of work to be done before they opened it up for business.

Alyssa walked out onto the back deck, breathing in the chilly mountain air. "I can't believe that I actually feel a little out of breath. We're only about a thousand feet higher than Salt Lake City here, aren't we?"

Lauren was standing beside her, looking out at the lake. "Yeah, but Salt Lake is high, too."

"That's true." Alyssa leaned on the deck after knocking the snow that clung to the railing away. "Just think. In another six weeks that lake is going to be filled with boats and people. I love that we can be here during the off-season, and I kind of hope we can help there to be no off-season. I think with our ideas for snowmobiles and cross-country skiing, this place can be hopping year-round."

"That's certainly the goal," Taylor said, stepping out to join them with Amanda on her heels. "I have so many ideas, and I want to make them all work right now! But first, I think we need to have the kitchen redone. I wish we could wait for Kayla, but if we want it done before tourist season, we need to act now."

"Very true." Alyssa knew they wanted to get things going soon. Getting tourists in there quickly would make them realize they'd done the right thing. "Do you want me to see if Hannah knows anyone? Or should I just put an ad online? She told me that there's a Bear Lake Classifieds on Facebook, and I could put something there."

"Ask Hannah. I'd rather get a recommendation of someone who would work hard for us than just stabbing in the dark."

"I will. I want to have supper with her tonight anyway. She took the night off so she could come over and we could talk. And we'll eat somewhere."

"Probably Coopers," Amanda said with a grin.

"Only if it won't make her crazy to eat at her place of employment on her night off." Alyssa pulled out her phone and looked at the time. It was already getting dark. "I need to call her and let her know we're here. Then we can figure out where to eat." She stepped back into the house and went to the living room, noting that the décor really needed to be updated as well as the kitchen. They wanted the latest appliances, not something that would break down.

"Hello?" Hannah said. "Please tell me you're in Richland."

"I'm at the lake house," Alyssa said. Hannah had grown up in a house a couple of streets over, and the two girls had met the summer before they both started kindergarten. From then on, as soon as the family made it to Richland, Alyssa had gone straight to Hannah's house, and they had been inseparable. Now it was hard to believe it had been five years since they'd seen each other in person.

"I'm on my way."

Alyssa looked at her phone, realizing Hannah had ended the call. No matter. She had moved a little further away, but she was still within a two-minute drive.

Alyssa hurried into the bathroom and ran a brush through her hair. A night out with Hannah was just what she needed. "I'll bring her back here right after supper," Alyssa called to her sisters, feeling a little guilty for abandoning them on their first night.

"We'll be here," Taylor said. "I'm walking through the house and figuring out what needs to be updated first. We have a lot to do, and we don't have much time to get it all done."

The doorbell rang, and Alyssa ran for the door, throwing it open. "Hannah!"

The two friends embraced. "I missed you so much," Hannah said, tears streaming. "I'm so sorry about your parents."

"Me too." Alyssa looked behind her and saw Lauren. "We'll be back after supper, and we'll all catch up."

Lauren nodded and watched as the two friends hurried out the door.

THIRTEEN

ALYSSA WAS SO happy to have time to spend with Hannah that she could barely contain herself. She hurried out and got into the passenger seat of her friend's old beat up pickup truck. If she remembered correctly, it was the same truck Hannah had driven when they were teens.

"Okay, so tell me all about where you are in the process of opening the bookstore." Alyssa turned to her friend as much as she could while buckled.

"It's slow going. I found a site, but we need to pour the concrete, and we can't do that until the ground is unfrozen." Hannah shrugged. "I have the money to do it all now—thanks to your parents—and I'm starting to work with an architect to draw out exactly what I'm looking for."

"So . . . when do you think you'll be able to open?" Alyssa hated that her friend was having to wait. It could be another six weeks before the snow was completely over for the year. Idaho was not known for early springs.

"It's probably going to be at least December. More likely in the spring. It depends on weather and all that good stuff. It's okay, though, because I'm no longer working a hundred hours a week to make it happen. Now we're waiting on Mother Nature to smile at me."

"That works, then. Where are we going for supper?" Alyssa asked.

"Oh, I'm taking you to Coopers. My treat! I want to sit and talk about nothing and everything."

"Two subjects that suit me just fine."

"So, tell me about the B&B. I love that you guys are doing it, but are all of you going to be part of running it?"

"Absolutely not. I'm still going to be a real estate agent. I love the work too much to give it up. I'm going to start studying for my test bright and early Wednesday morning." Alyssa couldn't imagine trying to make all the decisions that would need to be made if they all had to have a say in everything. "Taylor is going to manage the place, because she has the experience, and it was her idea. For now, I think Lauren is going to work with her, cleaning rooms and making breakfasts."

"Sounds good . . ." Hannah turned off the main road, heading toward the restaurant.

"Kayla is going to do maintenance for the house and any renovations that need to be done, but she plans on continuing flipping houses. I wouldn't be surprised if she quit selling them and started renting them out as Airbnbs, but she hasn't said those are the plans. Amanda is going to work her magic on the house, but she'll be hiring out for other jobs as well." Alyssa shrugged. "We'll all keep doing what we do best, but we'll be living together. At least in the beginning."

Hannah parked the truck, and they both hopped down. "I think that all makes a whole lot of sense. It would be hard for all of you to work together all the time as well as live together. I remember some major fights when you were up here every summer. It might be best to try to avoid those."

"You mean like the time Kayla got mad at Amanda and cut her hair while she was sleeping?"

Hannah laughed. "Exactly like that. Might be best that you're all going to have jobs outside of the B&B."

"Probably. I'm looking forward to exploring the area as an adult. I want to go to the ghost town between Soda and Lava. Chesterfield, I think? I want to go to the Oregon Trail Museum in Montpelier. I'm so excited to be back here where I've *always* felt like I belong."

"I'm just glad to have you back. It feels like it's been forever since we've just hung out together." Hannah looked as excited about their move as Alyssa felt.

"We were both working, and it's harder when you're an adult."

"It is." Hannah smiled at the hostess. "Two of us."

"Sure, this way." The girl led them to the back of the restaurant and around a corner. "This good?"

"Thanks, Maryann."

"No problem." Maryann hurried away, leaving them alone with their menus.

"I haven't been here in forever. Is the food the same as it used to be?" Alyssa asked.

"Nothing in Bear Lake ever changes. You know that as well as I do."

"Then I'm getting a bacon cheeseburger. I remember them from when I was a kid, and I loved them so much." Alyssa closed her menu and looked at her friend. "So, I want to know all there is to know about Hannah. Are you seeing anyone?"

"No one. I haven't really had time to date since high school. I was just working way too many hours to even think about it."

"That makes sense, I guess. You don't have your eye on anyone?" Alyssa hoped that having the money she needed would let Hannah slow down just a little. She hated to see her friend practically work herself to death.

Hannah laughed. "All I've had my eye on is the prize, and I'm so close to getting there now, I can taste it." She took a sip of the water that had been placed in front of both of them. "So, I'm surprised Tim let you move away."

Alyssa's eyes widened. "I didn't tell you? Tim and I broke up the day the will was read. Right after I talked to you on the phone actually. He came by, and I broke it off. And then he asked for money." Alyssa shook her head. "Taylor walked up behind me and closed the door on his foot. It was awesome."

Hannah grinned. "I so wish I'd been there to see that. I would have given his foot a good stomp. Would have gone well with the door closing on it."

"You know, that was a thought. I wish I'd come up with it at the time."

"And you haven't heard from him since?" Hannah asked.

"Oh, he stopped by the house once, and he's called a few times. I ignore it. I have nothing left to say to him. Nothing at all." Alyssa knew it was such a change for her after she'd done everything she could to become the woman he wanted her to be.

"What made you change your mind?"

Alyssa sighed, noticing the waitress was there. After they'd given their orders, she answered her friend's question. "When the police came and told me about Mom and Dad, I knew I needed to talk to someone right away. Someone who could be sympathetic without really knowing my parents. I needed an impartial person to just cry to."

"Well, yeah. I get that." Hannah took another sip of her water, wondering where this was all going.

"I called him, and he got onto me for calling so late, even though he was at a party. And he told me I should have called my sisters, like I was a stupid child. It still took my sisters ganging up on me and telling me to dump him to actually do it, but I did, and it's all over now." Alyssa leaned back in the hard, wooden chair. "I'm so glad I made the decision. Now I'm free to be here. Although . . . he probably would have liked it better if we'd stayed together, and I was here and he was there."

"Oh, that's awful. I hope you don't really believe that. How on earth did you end up with a jerk like him anyway?"

"He was so nice at first. And complimentary. I truly thought he was the man of my dreams, but it's obvious that I was wrong. And now I've opened my eyes and broken things off."

Hannah shook her head. "It's about time."

Alyssa wasn't sure how to respond to that, but she did know that Hannah had her best interests at heart. "Oh, I just remembered that my sisters wanted me to ask you if you knew of anyone who could help us with some remodeling stuff. Kayla had to stay in Salt Lake to finish the house she was working on, and she probably won't join us for at least another month. We would like to open on the first of June, so we have to move fast."

"You know what? I think I *do* know someone. He was a couple grades ahead of us in school, and I went out with him a few times, but there was absolutely no spark between us. His name is Nick Peot."

"Name doesn't ring a bell with me." Alyssa knew a lot of kids from the area simply because she'd spent so much time there. Not everyone, though.

"I'll have him give you a call in the morning. I know you'll be happy with his work, and he's very reasonable. Works hard to make his clients happy."

"Sounds like exactly what we're looking for. I was going to post in the Bear Lake Classifieds on Facebook, but I wanted someone who came with a recommendation. So, thanks for that."

After their meal, they went back to the lake house, and Hannah went in to see Alyssa's sisters. She was invited to sit with them in the living room, and they all reminisced for hours.

Finally, Hannah got to her feet to leave. "I know I'm not really working in the morning, but I do need to go see my architect. I keep requesting changes to his drawings, and I think I'm slowly driving him insane. I need what I need, though."

Alyssa walked her to the door, hugging her close. "Don't be a stranger. I feel like I just got my best friend back after a long walk through the desert. Or is it a long swim through the lake? Either way, I've missed you, and I'm glad I have you back."

"Welcome home, Alyssa. I hope you're as happy here as you've always dreamed you would be."

Alyssa smiled. "How could I not be with my best friend in the whole world right here with me?"

"You just remember that when you feel the need for a McDonald's burger. Or Chick-fil-A. We're sparse on places to eat out up here."

"If I feel that strong an urge, I'll put my butt in my car and drive to Logan. It's not *that* far."

"I hope you always feel that way." Hannah winked at her. "See you very soon. Maybe this weekend?"

"Sounds great. We'll grill out."

"Just let me know when, and I'll be here."

"Will do!" Alyssa watched Hannah hurry to her car and drive away before joining her sisters in the living room. "Being back here feels so right."

"That's because we're right back where we belong." Taylor sighed, putting her feet up on an ottoman. "We're living the lake life again."

FOURTEEN

Nick decided to go see Ryan at the hardware store to see if he had heard of any jobs he could do. There had been a few little ones in the past few weeks, but he needed something big. A kitchen remodel—or better yet a whole house—to sink his teeth into.

In the weeks since he'd kicked Kami out, he only felt relief. She'd picked her things up from his front porch on the specified day, and he'd only gotten to burn the pictures of the two of them together. He would have preferred to burn everything she owned, but she'd taken that option away from him. She'd taken a lot of options away from him in their time together.

He hadn't worked since the Friday before, and it was Tuesday. Sure, that was only a three-day weekend, but it was more time off than he'd had in a while, and he was desperate to get paint under his fingernails. For him, it wasn't about the money—well, not all about the money anyway. The work revitalized him and kept him going.

He was halfway to the hardware store to talk to Ryan when a call came in. Pressing a button, he answered it hands-free in his truck. "Hello?"

"Hey, Nick. It's Hannah. My dearest friend and her sisters just moved to the lake, and they want to fix up their house to turn it into a B&B. One of the younger sisters has the knowledge and ability, but she's not going to join for a month or two. You interested?"

"Definitely. What's the house?" He didn't even have to hear where it was to get excited. He wanted to do this. It sounded like the kind of big project that would be good for him.

"The Romriell house. I'm sure you've heard talk of them. Summer people at the lake, and they want to make it into the best B&B in the area."

Nick grinned. "I've never been on the inside, but that house is *amazing*. I saw that they poured concrete. Is that for a parking lot?"

"It is. You should head over there today. My friend and three of her sisters are there."

"None of them are going to come onto me, are they?" he asked. He didn't want to think about being in a house alone with four women. After his recent experience, the very idea turned his stomach.

Hannah laughed. "No, they won't. Head on over, and see who's there. My friend is Alyssa if you want someone to ask to talk to. Otherwise talk to whomever opens the door. They're all part of this."

"All right." Nick made a three-point turn and headed back toward the Romriell house. His hands were already itching to get started. The house was amazing, and he was sure anything that he could do to make it better would thrill him *and* the women. "I'm on my way."

"You want her cell number?" she asked.

"Nah, I'm driving. I'll just stop in." He didn't have far to go, and within minutes he was parking in the driveway of the biggest house in Richland. A house that dreams were made of.

When he rang the bell, he had to wait for a minute before a young brunette came to the door. She stared at him for a moment, confusion on her face. "What can I help you with?"

"I hear you're turning this place into a B&B. I was told to come talk to Alyssa." Nick hoped she'd just let him in, because he was dying to see the house, but she stood there for a minute, just looking at him.

"Lauren, who's here?" a voice from behind the young woman—Lauren—asked.

"Some guy who says he's supposed to talk to you about turning the house into a B&B. I didn't know we'd even contacted anyone!" Lauren said, still looking at him skeptically.

Nick smiled. "Hannah told me to come by."

"Oh!" Lauren was gently pushed out of the way, and another brunette—older and prettier than the last—was looking at him. "Hannah told me she'd have someone call me. I wasn't expecting you to just show up. I'm Alyssa." She offered her hand to shake, and he noticed then she was in a robe that was tied tightly in front of her. "We just moved in yesterday, so it's still a bit of a mess, but come in, and we'll talk about what we want to do." Alyssa looked over at Lauren, who was still standing there looking at him, a pancake turner in her hand. "I'll get the others. *You* entertain him."

Lauren frowned at him. "How do you want me to entertain you? I could do a little song and dance or something."

Alyssa turned just before starting up a beautifully curved flight of stairs. "Lauren!"

"Fine." Lauren pasted a smile on her face. "Come in. I'll show you to the living room, and we'll sit and chat about the weather, because I'm not sure what anyone wants done yet, and then when my sisters get here to talk to you, they can tell me to run along and play."

Stepping into a huge foyer, Nick was amazed already. The tile and intricate woodwork fascinated him. He could put a counter along one wall to greet and check in guests, and it wouldn't even begin to feel cramped. He wanted to start measuring immediately, but he wasn't sure how Lauren would react, and she was obviously in charge of him for the next little bit.

Nick laughed. "You must be the youngest."

"You got that right." Lauren led him to a spacious living room with a large screen television against one wall and more seating than he would have thought necessary for a family. "Have a seat."

He sat down, leaning back against the cushions for a moment. Whatever they were doing with the place, they needed to keep the couch. It was the most comfortable piece of furniture he'd been on in ages. "You don't really have to entertain me. Finish making your breakfast. I'll play with my phone."

"That would be great. I don't mean to be rude, but I was about to start making some scrambled eggs for my sisters and myself, and then the doorbell rang, completely throwing me off course. Sit here, and someone will be here soon." Lauren rushed from the room, twirling the utensil in her hand.

Instead of sitting like a good boy, Nick wandered around the room, studying the walls and the structure of the building. He was even more excited to start now that he was inside. Hopefully he'd get the job, though he didn't know exactly what the women were hoping for. If it meant working in that house, he wanted to do it.

He was looking at a built-in bookshelf when he heard someone clear their throat behind them. "I guess Lauren abandoned you?"

"I told her I was capable of taking care of myself, and that's what I'm doing. This house is absolutely amazing." Nick turned around to see Alyssa watching him.

She smiled. "I've always thought so. My sisters will be down in a minute." She waved a hand toward the sofa again. "I'd love to start by telling you a little about what we're wanting to do here, if you don't mind."

"I don't mind at all." He sat down, smiling when she did the same. He was a little disappointed that she'd changed her robe for sweat pants and a t-shirt, but he'd have to adjust.

"This house was built by our parents shortly after I was born so they would have a place to escape Salt Lake City during summers. They made sure it was big enough for all of our aunts, uncles, and cousins. There are six bedrooms and seven bathrooms on each floor. We're going to want each bedroom to have a lock installed on the door—to which we'll retain a master key—and we want to make certain that each bathroom is in good working order. While the construction work is being done, my four sisters and I will be living in the house. Well, three sisters until we're joined by Kayla, who is the only one of us who has any construction skills or experience. She is a house flipper, but she's not finished with the house she's working on, so she will be here when she is."

"I see." He studied the woman across from him carefully. She was beautiful, and he wanted to ask if she came with the house, but after Kami, he was a little too skittish around beautiful women for that. "So, you want the bathrooms redone?"

"We want to start with the kitchen," she said. "It is a great kitchen, but it hasn't been redone since it was built in the early nineties. My sisters and I haven't had much chance to talk about exactly what we're looking for, but my sister Amanda is an interior designer, and I know she went through the house last night making some notes."

"Yes, I did," said another feminine voice, and Nick's eyes gravitated to yet another beautiful brunette. The Romriell girls were all lookers. There was no doubt about that. "I'm Amanda." She walked in and sat down on a chair, pulling out a notebook. "The first order of business is definitely the kitchen. We want a commercial dishwasher installed, and I have marked the one I'm interested in. If you can't get it at a discount through your suppliers, then I can through mine. We want the old, ugly linoleum taken out and ceramic tile to take its place. The walls need a new coat of paint—in a more appealing color —and I'd like the cabinets ripped out and new ones put in. I've drawn up what I'm looking for in each of those things. We'll also need a new six-burner stove and a new wall oven. A kitchen island with a sink in it, so two of us can work on meals at once. There are a few other things, but that's the beginning. Are you capable of doing all of that?"

He smiled. "I most certainly am. I'd love to see the kitchen." He hoped they'd let him start immediately. This was the kind of project he'd been practicing for his entire career.

Alyssa shook her head. "I think Nick here has designs on our home."

"I definitely do. I've seen this house a million times growing up in town, and I always wanted to see the inside. Now I'm seeing it, and I want to touch everything, and . . ." Nick shrugged. "I love this house."

"We do, too," Amanda said. "That's why we want to make sure you're the right man for the job."

Alyssa looked over at Amanda. "Did you and Taylor go over everything last night? Is there anything she thinks is more important to start out?"

Amanda shook her head. "We went over it, and she's happy with my plans. She also wants a commercial washer and dryer, but that won't be in Nick's realm."

Yet another sister walked in then, and Nick was starting to get a little nervous. There was no way he was going to be able to tell them all apart. Their hair was the same shade. Alyssa had big brown eyes, though, and the others had lighter eyes. At least he could pick her out from the others. "That's right. I'm very onboard with Amanda's plans. I think she's got great taste. I just wish we could agree on a theme for the guest rooms." She sat down in yet another chair and looked at him. Nick felt a bit like he was surrounded.

"That works. When do we want to get started?"

"Today," Taylor said emphatically. "Are you currently working a job?"

"I finished one Friday. I'm happy to start whenever you're ready for me." Nick was excited, thanking God this had dropped into his lap when it did. He still couldn't believe his good fortune. He was willing to do anything he had to do to get this job.

"Let's have you work a bid up on the kitchen, then. We don't have unlimited funds to make this happen," Alyssa said, getting to her feet and leading him toward the kitchen.

When Nick stepped into the kitchen, he couldn't help but smile. The room was huge, with a table for eight at one end and seemingly endless cabinets and counterspace. "Are we leaving the counters as is?"

"I'd prefer granite counter tops," Amanda said, stopping next to Lauren. "That smells good. What are you making?"

"I call it breakfast!" Lauren said as her sisters and the contractor swarmed her in the kitchen.

"Good choice," Alyssa said with a grin. "Coffee?"

"In the pot. I started that first thing."

Alyssa helped herself to a mug. "Coffee?" she asked Nick.

"Sounds good."

She poured two mugs of coffee, obviously not caring if her sisters had to get their own. "What do you think?"

"Give me an hour to check on some prices, and I'll give you an estimate. If I only supply labor, I can give you a cheaper price . . ."

"I'll handle the supplies, then," Amanda said. "I have suppliers in Salt Lake, and to save the money, I can drive down and get the materials if that makes things easier."

"It probably would." Nick looked around slowly as he sipped his coffee. "I'm going to need to take some measurements and make some notes." He looked at Amanda. "I'm assuming you want custom cabinets?"

"Yes, absolutely. Can you build them yourself, or will you need to farm that out?"

"Oh, I can do that myself. No problem at all." He smiled. "Can I get started measuring now?"

"After breakfast," Lauren said. "You're eating with us, because I made extra."

Nick grinned. He had left the cabin without breakfast that morning, having gotten into the habit of eating from a gas station with Kami living there. "That would be wonderful."

Together, the five of them sat down to eat, and Nick only felt a little out of place. His eyes were on the remodel he would do, and he was thinking about exactly what the work would entail. He'd eaten two bites before he couldn't hold back his next question. "When do you want the kitchen done by?"

Amanda and Taylor exchanged a look. "We'd like to have it done within the next two weeks. We have a lot of work that needs to be done before we can open the B&B, and we're hoping to be able to open by June first."

He choked a bit on his coffee. "June first? I'm not sure that's possible."

"How long do you think the kitchen will take, then?" Amanda asked. She wasn't going to back down on what they needed to change. If they were going to run a business out of the house, they had to be equipped for it.

"Three weeks if I hurry? Do you object to paying a little extra for a rush job? I can work weekends if that'll help you, but no days off might make for a grumpy Nick."

"Grumpy or not, if you get the work done properly, we'll be happy." Alyssa took a bite of her scrambled eggs. "Now you understand why we want you to start immediately."

"I do." He took a deep breath. "As soon as breakfast is over, I'll get an estimate worked up. I'd like to start immediately after lunch, if possible." He was pretty sure the job was his, because he'd been recommended by Hannah, but more importantly, he was there, and no one else was. He needed to get to work right away.

"Sounds good." Alyssa seemed a little off to him, and he wasn't sure why. She was a beautiful woman, but something was going on there. "I'm going for a run after breakfast. I trust my sisters to be here with you while I do."

Lauren frowned at Alyssa, and Nick couldn't help but wonder why. "A run?"

"I've discovered in the past few years that I *love* to run, though I don't love lifting weights. So, I'm going to continue my runs." Alyssa shrugged, sipping her coffee. "And I'm the oldest, so you don't get to worry about me."

"Try and stop me." Lauren grinned at Alyssa.

"That goes double for me," Taylor said softly.

"You're not leaving me out," Amanda said. "Sisters worry about sisters, and it doesn't matter who is the oldest and who is the youngest. That's just how it works."

"I guess it is." Alyssa took another sip of her coffee and stood up. "I'll be back in thirty minutes or so. I might run along the beach."

"There's not much of a beach right now. It's just snow. I would stick to the roads if I were you." Nick felt the need to warn her.

Alyssa made a face. "I might need to have a treadmill here. That will keep me running no matter the time of year." With those words, she disappeared out the front door, and Nick had to wonder why the others were worried when she went for a run. Seemed to him that running was good for a person.

FIFTEEN

As soon as Alyssa was outside the house, she breathed a sigh of relief. Her hormones were in a whirl after meeting Nick. She was a million times more attracted to the man than she had ever been to Tim, and spending time with the contractor was the last thing she needed. He was certainly good-looking, but it was more than that. Her instinct was to run from him, because she couldn't deal with another relationship with a man like Tim. She almost wanted to refuse whatever bid he gave them, just so she could avoid him, but contractors weren't that plentiful in Bear Lake. If his quote was good, they would have no choice but to accept it.

She did wish her sisters hadn't made a fuss about her running in front of him, because it was none of his business why they didn't think she should run. All of her sisters had expressed to her—privately—that they were worried she was becoming anorexic after the time with Tim. She didn't think so, but she had to respect their worries. Still, she would have preferred if they hadn't spoken so freely in front of Nick.

She stretched a little and started a slow jog down toward the lake, which was one of their property borders. She could see that Nick had been right, and there was no beach, only snow, so she decided to keep her run on the streets of the small town. It wouldn't be as fun, but she could run on the beach all summer long. She hoped. It had been known to snow in Bear Lake in June.

Her favorite thing about running was allowing her thoughts to roam freely. She never tried to direct her brain to certain thoughts, and instead it was whatever jumped to the forefront. Alyssa knew a lot of people who preferred to run with an audiobook or music playing, but that kept her from what she needed.

Being back in the small town was wonderful. She remembered each street well. Running past the house where Hannah had grown up, she smiled. They had spent a lot of time playing at her house so her cousins and sisters wouldn't bother them.

Next, she ran past the shake place where Bear Lake raspberry shakes were made and sold. It had been a thing when they were kids to walk over there every day for a raspberry shake. Of course, Kayla had always insisted on chocolate shakes, which made no sense to Alyssa. Chocolate shakes were everywhere. Only in Bear Lake could you get raspberry shakes—or better yet, raspberry cheesecake shakes—to keep your taste buds jumping. She noted that the shake shack was closed until Memorial Day and frowned. They would have to figure out how to make raspberry shakes on their own. It was too much a highlight of being at the lake to miss out during the spring and winter.

She kept running, moving on toward the elementary school. All the kids in the area went to this little school, but for junior high and high school, they were bused over to Montpelier like all the other kids in the country.

She made a full circle around the elementary school and headed back toward the house, not sure if she was ready to be finished. Glancing down at her Apple Watch, she saw that she'd only gone one point two miles, and she wanted to do a full four miles before she was done.

And she didn't want to do it because it had anything to do with her weight. It was for her health, and it just felt good to run. Despite what she'd always thought, when it became a habit, she actually started to enjoy it. She hadn't run much in the past few weeks as she'd dealt with the fallout of her parents' deaths and the decisions they'd made following them. Now she realized that she'd needed to have this time with her thoughts flowing freely.

Every car she passed had a driver who waved at her, which was one of her favorite things about the small town. No one was a stranger to anyone, and eventually, she and her sisters would be considered locals and not just summer people.

As she ran, she glanced at houses, noting when there was a "For Sale" sign. There were so many different homes for sale in the area, and she knew most would end up being Airbnbs if they didn't get purchased by someone in the area. She could be someone purchasing a home in a month or two. The lake house would be a place she could always visit, but living with her sisters, though enjoyable for the short term, was not something she could do forever.

Finally, she turned down the street to go right back home, and she smiled at the word. Home. She really did feel like she was finally home.

She didn't go to the front door, and instead she went around back to the deck, knowing she wanted to sauna before she joined the others. She wanted to kick herself for not remembering to preheat the thing before she started running, but it didn't matter. Today was about reacquainting herself with the community and getting her things unpacked.

Alyssa walked to the sauna to turn it on, thinking she was going to have to go to the kitchen for some water anyway, when she noticed someone had heated it up for her. Not only was it on, there were three bottles of water lying on the cover of the hot tub. All of them had water dripping down the sides, so she knew they were cold.

She smiled, stripping down to her underwear. One of her sisters had definitely thought of her. She would have to remember to thank them when she was finished.

Getting into the sauna, she set the egg timer they kept on the bench in there for twenty minutes. At first, the heat actually felt good after the cold from her run, but it didn't take five minutes before she was feeling too hot for comfort. She drank the bottles of water and wished she'd thought to bring her e-reader in. If she kept a bottle of cold water touching it at all times, she was sure the e-reader could be kept from over-heating.

The sauna was a decent size, meant for six people. Her parents and aunts and uncles had used it a lot when she was growing up, and she'd always thought they were crazy for cooking themselves. Since, she'd done research on the benefits of using a sauna for twenty minutes six days a week, and she'd wished she had access to one. Well, now she did. She was sure she'd mentioned to Amanda that she was looking forward to using the sauna after exercising. It was probably her who had preheated it and left the water.

When she got out, she shut the sauna off along with the light before putting her sweaty clothes back on. She went up the stairs to the bedroom she'd chosen for its view of the lake, and she stripped, getting into the shower.

At that moment, she realized that this was her perfect morning routine for the lake. She'd eat, run, sauna, and then shower. Then she would start the studying she needed to do to get her real estate license transferred to Idaho. She'd already set up her test for May seventh, so she only had about three weeks to prepare, but that should be more than long enough.

Once she was dressed in jeans and a hoodie, she went back downstairs, wondering if there was a bid yet. Surely Nick had enough time to get one ready for them.

Nick. Even his name made her heart beat faster. She sighed. That was not what she needed right now. She'd focused way too much on her relationship with Tim for the last seven years, and she was done with men for a while. It was time for her to focus on herself instead.

She went into the kitchen, where her sisters were looking over a piece of paper while Nick was looking more closely at the entryway of the house. "So, let me see."

Amanda handed her the paper, and Alyssa blanched at the total for just the kitchen, but she knew Amanda knew a great deal more about what it should cost to do the work than she did. "Is that a good price?"

Amanda nodded. "It's about half of what we'd pay for labor in Salt Lake. People here just work cheaper." She shrugged. "Now I want you to keep in mind that with materials, we're looking at double this cost, and I'll be driving to Salt Lake for the materials. All he's charging us for is his labor."

"Wow." Alyssa looked at Taylor and Lauren. "What do you two think?"

Taylor shrugged. "Amanda says it's a good deal, and I trust her. He said he'd do the work in three weeks, and that sounds reasonable. He'll be building cabinets off-site to get them ready to put in."

"Lauren?" Alyssa asked.

Lauren shrugged. "I think I know less about this than anyone else in this room. If you three all agree, then I agree, too."

Amanda smiled at that. "I say we do it. He can get started ripping out cabinets and tearing up that ugly linoleum this morning. I'll place the order with my supplier in Salt Lake, and I'll plan to head down to pick up the supplies tomorrow. He said he'd carry them in if we fetch them. He offered to go get them, too, but I don't want him to miss a day of work when we need him so badly."

Alyssa nodded. "That makes a lot of sense to me. Who is going with you? I don't want you driving more than five hours round-trip tomorrow on your own."

Amanda rolled her eyes. "Taylor? Lauren?"

Lauren nodded. "I think Taylor should be here to keep doing her bookkeeping stuff and getting all of our ducks in a row. I'm expendable, so I'll go and help. My liberal arts degree in action!"

"Sounds good. I'd volunteer, but I want to start my studying for the Idaho test in the morning. I'll probably run through neighborhoods again. I'm trying to get a good feel for the real estate market in the area." Alyssa leaned back against the counter, pulling some Junior Mints from the pocket of her hoodie and popping a couple in her mouth. When she noticed Amanda smiling, she frowned at her. "What?"

"I just think you're hilarious with the running and then the partaking of Junior Mints so close together." Amanda was obviously thrilled to see her eating the sweets.

Alyssa shook her head, laughing. "I keep telling you guys, I *don't have a problem.* I just like to run, and if I keep up my running schedule, Junior Mints will never be a problem." She turned and saw that Nick had returned. "You're hired. Amanda's ordering what you'll need, and she and Lauren will drive down tomorrow to pick it up. We will still need to be able to cook in here some, so try not to destroy the entire kitchen."

"There'll be a few days where cooking is out of the question if you want it done that quickly," Nick warned her.

"I guess we'll eat out those days. We'll figure something out. What can we do to help you get started?"

He grinned. "Just stay out of the kitchen for now. I'll go get my crowbar and get to work." He was halfway out of the kitchen when he stopped short. "I really appreciate the opportunity to work on this house. It was kind of a beacon for all of us who grew up in the area, and it feels special."

"Make sure you keep our trust," Alyssa said. "Hannah has complete faith in you, or you wouldn't be given the chance." She reached for a few more Junior Mints as he nodded and left the house.

"That was a little harsh," Lauren said. "Why be rude?"

"I wasn't being rude. I was setting realistic expectations. If he wants to complete the renovation of the entire house, he needs to do a good job on the kitchen. Plain and simple."

"Felt harsh." Lauren headed for the stairs. "I'm going to go and read a cookbook or two. I want to make orange muffins for breakfast in the morning. That way I'm earning my keep."

"You're family. You don't need to earn your keep!" Taylor called after her.

"Sure, I do. Everyone else has a job to do every day. My turn!" Lauren disappeared up the stairs, leaving the other three sisters standing there together.

"Now, about themes for our guest rooms . . ." Amanda said. "I don't want just boring guest rooms. Themes are important to me."

"What do you have in mind?" Taylor asked.

Nick came back in then, and the three of them headed into the living room.

"Let's finish this in here, so we're not in the way," Alyssa said. "What ideas do you have? I want it to be something that's unique and not overdone."

"Well, I thought Broadway musicals could be fun. Each room with a different theme. Or we could do famous fictional lovers. Like Rhett and Scarlett or Anne and Gilbert or Elizabeth Bennet and Mr. Darcy or even Ross and Rachel." Amanda shrugged. "I would love those ideas, but would everyone?"

"We could do Disney movies or famous actors and actresses, too," Taylor suggested.

"All of that would work. Taylor, what do you think would keep people coming back? You're the expert on all that stuff," Alyssa said.

Taylor thought for a moment. "Maybe we could do famous books," she suggested. "Then we could do famous couples, but also have some whimsy thrown in. Do a *Gone with the Wind* room and a *Harry Potter* room. You know kids would go nuts for the Harry Potter room if they were coming with their parents."

"Oh, I like that!" Amanda said. "I have goosebumps." She held her arm out to show her sisters.

"Me too!" Alyssa said. "A *Sherlock Holmes* room and a *Carrie* room with blood trickling down the walls."

Taylor shook her head. "No way are we doing Carrie, you psychopath."

"I'm not a psychopath. I'm using my creative energy here. Sorry you don't like a perfectly legitimate idea." Alyssa stuck her tongue out at her sister, realizing they could reduce her to childish behavior faster than anyone else on the planet.

All three of them laughed. "Could be fun," Amanda said. "I'm going to get started, and I'll make a list. When the list is completed, we'll do a Facetime call with Kayla, and we'll each get to vote for seven room themes."

"Perfect. That was easy," Alyssa said with a grin.

"Easy for you to say," Amanda said, shaking her head. "I've been wrestling with this for weeks."

"No more wrestling. Write down ideas, and we'll make it happen." Taylor grinned. "I can't believe we're going to have our very own bed and breakfast."

"We'll have to throw out names for it on that call as well," Alyssa said. "We can't just call it the bed and breakfast forever."

"Good idea. I'll make a note of that." Taylor pulled a notebook she'd taken to carrying everywhere with her from her pocket. "We'll talk about this on the call. Let's plan for Saturday. I'll contact Kayla and check her schedule."

"Perfect. We're going to totally rock the bed and breakfast market." Amanda got to her feet. "And now I'm going to go and make my order. Then they'll have it ready when we get there tomorrow."

The excitement in Amanda's eyes was reflected in Taylor's as well. Alyssa had to wonder if her eyes held the same excitement, but she thought they probably did. This was the first thing she'd been truly excited about doing in a very long time.

SIXTEEN

NICK GRINNED to himself as he knelt on the floor in the kitchen of the Romriell house. He loved listening to the sisters talk about their plans and goals for the place. He could *feel* the excitement in the air surrounding them. This was the type of project he'd wanted to do for a very long time, but he'd never really had the chance.

The sisters intrigued him. All of them . . . but to him the *most* intriguing was Alyssa. She was the oldest, but the others seemed to be protecting her from something. It was strange.

Still, he was very excited to be part of this project, following what they were thinking about. Amanda had given him some rough sketches of what she was looking for in the way of cabinets, and then she'd provided him with pictures as well. If all of the sisters were as focused and clear about what they were looking for, he had a feeling they would get along just fine.

When lunchtime rolled around, he went in search of one of the sisters—any of the sisters—so he could let them know he was leaving for lunch. He hadn't realized he'd be starting a job that day, or he'd have brought his lunch with him.

He found Alyssa in the living room with a laptop on her lap. "Alyssa?" he said.

"Yeah." She glanced up from her computer, giving him her complete attention.

He liked knowing she was actually listening to him. Kami had spent all of her time looking at some screen and never really paying any attention to him. It made him crazy. "I'm going to head out to grab some lunch. I'll be bringing my lunch from now on, but I didn't know I'd be starting a project today."

Alyssa frowned. "Why don't I run and get lunch for the both of us? That way you don't need to stop working for quite as long, and I can learn my way around better."

"That would be great. I was thinking about just grabbing a burger. The Burger Hut is open. Down on Main."

She nodded. "What do you like on your burgers?"

"Everything. Get me a double cheeseburger and a large onion ring. A Dr. Pepper to go with it." He would have rather gone with her so they could chat as they ate, but he knew better. He needed to steer clear of women for a little while, and he was already comparing this one to Kami. That wasn't a good sign.

"All right. I'll be back in a flash."

Nick watched as she headed out the door and returned to his project ripping up floors. He needed to limit his alone time with that sister. The others didn't bother him like she did. The woman already held some kind of power over him, and he didn't need to mess with her.

She was back a short while later with four bags of food and a soft drink. She walked into the dining room with them, and he followed his nose. "Thank you for getting me lunch. How much was mine?"

Alyssa shook her head. "Don't worry about it. I got lunch for my sisters and myself as well, and I have no idea how much one meal was." She walked to an intercom button on the wall in the dining room. "Hey everyone. I've got lunch. Meet me in the dining room."

She dug through the sacks and pulled out his double cheeseburger with onion rings, handing it to him. "The drink is yours as well." She wandered out of the dining room and came back a moment later with a couple of two liters, one Coke and one Sprite. She had a pile of red Solo cups on top of the Coke bottle, and she immediately opened it and poured herself a glass.

The sisters came in one after the other, each of them plopping down on a chair at the formal dining table.

"Thanks for being willing to not eat in the kitchen for a little while," he said, happy that they were respecting his need for keeping the kitchen off-limits while he tore things up.

"No problem," Alyssa said, dumping out fries and onion rings onto a couple of paper plates and liberally squirting from a bottle of fry sauce onto each of the plates. "None of us have any desire to eat dust anyway."

Obviously, the sisters all ate their burgers the same, because they each just grabbed one and used the paper as a plate. Then they shared the fries and onion rings, each of them seeming to eat from both plates. It was interesting to watch them eating together as if they'd done it a thousand times before, and he was sure they had. He didn't have a sibling of his own, so he'd always been fascinated by large family dynamics.

"How's it coming?" Amanda asked him. "Find anything strange we should know about?"

He shook his head. "Nope. It's all going perfectly and as expected." He took a swallow of his Dr. Pepper. "I should have the floors up by the end of the day, and I'll start on the cabinets if there's time. I guess I should tell you that I'm going to be around here a whole lot while we get the kitchen done. I'll be here by seven every morning and working until seven or so. You're all going to be sick of me soon."

Alyssa tilted her head to one side. "If you're going to be working that many hours, we can at least provide snacks for you. Tell me what you'd like us to keep around, and we'll do it."

Nick shook his head. "You don't have to do that."

"Sure, we do. We're insisting the work is done quickly, which is going to be making you work ridiculous hours. It's the least we can do."

He'd never had anyone keep snacks around for him before, but it felt good that she'd offered. He listed a few things that would be easy to eat while he continued working, and she nodded. "I'll make sure they're here for you tomorrow."

"Thanks. I appreciate it." Nick finished the last bite of his burger. "I'm going to head back to work. Thanks for the lunch."

"No problem." Alyssa said, tapping his snack requests into her phone.

As he got back to work, Nick realized that the job he was doing for these women was going to keep him busy for a long time. They'd already said that if they kept him on for the bedrooms, they didn't all have to be done by June first. No, those could be finished one room at a time, and that suited him just fine. There was enough to do without having them all done on time.

As he worked, he wondered which books the sisters would choose to base their rooms on. He couldn't wait to find out. Their excitement with the project was contagious, and he was right there with them.

SEVENTEEN

THE FOLLOWING WEEK, the kitchen was closed to the sisters. The floor was torn up, the cabinets were out, and the entire room was being painted a mint green that set off the flecks of color in the tiles Amanda had chosen.

Alyssa spent more time than she should have studying for her test, but she made sure she checked on Nick at least five or six times during the day. She didn't know why she was so drawn to the man, but she couldn't seem to help herself.

There was no refrigerator, and the stove had been taken out. The kitchen had been completely gutted to make room for the changes they were making. It felt strange to see it that way, and she tried not to imagine her mom's face if she saw her kitchen at that moment.

She still went for her run every morning, but she wasn't moving nearly enough throughout the rest of the day, and she knew it. She needed to fix it, but until she was finished studying for her real estate license, she wouldn't be able to change things much. Studying had to be her first priority.

Nick had started timing his coffee break with the time she returned from her run every morning. He would bring them each a mug of coffee and whatever sweet treat he found sitting on the dining room table. They always seemed to have cookies or donuts or muffins around.

She'd just returned from her run for the day, and she was settling on the couch to reach for her laptop and start her daily studies when Nick walked into the room, a mug in each hand and a box of cookies stuck under one arm.

"It'll be nice when Hannah opens the bookstore. She's planning on having someone there baking cookies and cakes all day. Then we can get fresh cookies," he said, handing her a mug of coffee.

"Or we can just wait for Lauren to start making cookies and muffins every day, which she certainly plans to do if you ever finish the kitchen." She hid her grin with the coffee mug.

"Sure, blame the contractor for the lack of fresh baked goods in the house." He shook his head. "Why do I take coffee breaks with you again?"

"Penchant for punishment?" she asked.

"That must be it." He set the cookies on the couch between them and rubbed the back of his neck. "You know, I love that you girls are painting things exciting colors and not just white or off-white. Those colors are fine, of course, but they're not interesting. When I walk around wearing white paint, no one notices. Now people can see me coming."

"No one else around here paints using colors? Really?"

"Some people do, I guess. Kami never let me, and I always found that really annoying." Nick shook his head, reaching for one of the cookies.

"Kami?" Alyssa asked. He wasn't married, was he? How could that have escaped her notice?

"Oh, I forget you're not from around here. Kami was my fiancée until a couple of months ago." He shook his head. "I had already decided she wasn't the right woman for me, and I was just waiting for the right time to break things off. One day, I got home from work and found her . . . in a delicate position with another man."

"Oh! That's terrible!"

He shrugged. "It would have been a whole lot worse if I'd been in love with her, but I already knew it wasn't a good idea to marry her. She wasn't right for me, if that makes sense."

"Makes perfect sense. I think we all have people like that in our pasts." Alyssa reached for a cookie, and their fingers collided as he was getting another. She drew her hand back as if it had been burned. "Sorry."

"Don't be. All you have to do is tell me you want to hold hands, and I'm happy to oblige," he told her with a wink. Eating one last cookie, he drained his mug and got to his feet. "Same time tomorrow?"

She nodded, not quite meeting his eyes. "Sounds good to me. Coffee is what I always need right after that run."

"I'll bring more!" He sauntered out of the room, and she took a deep breath. She was already counting down the hours until their next coffee break.

Early the following afternoon, Alyssa took a break from her studying to go check out the work Nick was doing. Walking to the spot where the hallway met the kitchen, she looked in as Nick was stretching, his muscles showing well under his tight t-shirt. The shirt was obviously what he always painted in, because it was splattered with paint in an entire rainbow of colors, though it had once been royal blue with the words, "Bears" written across it for the Bear Lake Bears.

"How's it coming?" she asked softly from the edge of the room, afraid to walk in and disturb him too much. She had no desire to be as covered in paint as he was.

He turned and smiled at her. "Going good, I think. I should have the painting done today, and I'll start putting in the cabinets tomorrow. I've been building them at home, getting them ready. I've already got them stained."

"I can't wait to see them."

"I hope you ladies love them as much as I do. I made the kind that roll out so you have more storage space. It's what Amanda told me she wanted."

"Sounds good to me. It'll be fun to cook in here when it's all nice and pretty and functional." Alyssa didn't have a clear picture of what the room would look like as her sister did, but she was sure she'd love the finished result. Amanda was amazing at what she did.

She took a step into the room, walking past where the island had been, and didn't watch where she was going as well as she should have. She tripped over a paint tray that was setting in the middle of the floor, her eyes only on him.

She felt herself falling and let out a little squeal as she was caught in strong, masculine arms. Suddenly she was out of breath, and she knew it wasn't her near fall. No, it was the strong arms that were wrapped around her. She couldn't stay that close to him and still be able to breathe. It wasn't physically possible.

He helped steady her, keeping his arms around her for a moment longer than he should have. Her eyes met his, and she felt her heart skip a beat. She wanted to kick herself. This was the first man she'd spent any real time around since she'd broken things off with Tim, and she shouldn't be falling for him. She giggled a little as she thought the words, realizing they had a double meaning.

"Thank you for catching me."

He grinned, pulling her just a little closer. "Thank you for needing to be caught."

She blushed, stepping back. "I should get back to my studies."

"Is that what you're doing in there on that computer? What are you studying for?" he asked.

"I'm getting my real estate license for Idaho as well as Utah. I want to be able to buy and sell homes all over Bear Lake. I was a real estate agent in Salt Lake City for several years before we moved here." She didn't mention how successful she was at her career, because she didn't want him to think she was bragging.

"I think you need a study break, and I know I need a break, too. Take a walk with me."

Alyssa considered it for a moment, but she shook her head. "I really shouldn't." She couldn't get attached to a man yet. She wasn't ready. If she walked with him, what was to keep her from losing her heart completely?

"I know you run every morning, but you spend the rest of the day sitting. I know the paint fumes aren't good for you. Walk with me. Get some fresh air." Nick smiled, and a dimple stood out on his cheek. "Sitting is the new smoking, you know. At least that's what I keep hearing."

She bit her lip, worried about herself as she actually considered walking with him. "All right."

His whole face lit up in a grin. "Hopefully this cold snap will end soon." He frowned out the window where a light snow was falling. "It's almost May."

"I know. But at least the snow here is pretty and doesn't look like someone dumped dirt all over it." She went to the closet in the front entryway, grabbing her coat. She could do without mittens, but a coat was definitely called for at that moment.

He grabbed his own coat from the closet, where he'd been invited to hang it on his second day there. "Let's go."

He held the door open for her, and she stepped out in front of him, noting that his hand immediately went to her elbow. She remembered seeing a man help a woman that way on her last date with Tim, and she'd hoped Tim would someday learn to be just as gentlemanly. But here was a man who already knew how. He didn't even need to be taught.

Together, they walked down toward the lake. This was a new snowfall, and there was no standing snow, so they didn't have to worry about trudging through it on their way down to the lake. "I can't believe you came here every summer and we never met. I've known Hannah since we were both in elementary school."

Alyssa nodded. "It does seem odd, but I think you were a couple years ahead of us, from what Hannah said." She and Hannah had spent some time together over the weekend, and she had asked a few questions about Nick. She shouldn't have, because she needed a break from men, but she couldn't resist. Nick filled her mind whether he was there or not.

"Yeah. I was a senior when she was a sophomore. You two were in the same grade?"

"Yeah. We met the summer before we both started kindergarten. I think we played together every single day that summer. Her mother would come over and watch the two of us play in the water. I think they liked having the private beach access." Alyssa could still remember playing with Hannah that way. They'd built so many sandcastles.

Nick smiled. "Your mom didn't watch you?"

"Never. Hannah was the youngest in her family, so it was easy for her mom to watch us. She just had those two brothers who were tons older than her. My mom had Taylor and Amanda at that point, and if I remember right, she was expecting Kayla."

"I haven't met Kayla yet. She's a house flipper, right?"

"She is. She'll be at least another three weeks, but I'm sure we'll have the two of you work together when she gets here. There's no way she can do so much on her own that quickly." Alyssa stopped on the sand right in front of the edge of the water, feeling the snow landing on her face. "I love snow so much more here than I do in Salt Lake City."

He laughed. "Everything is prettier here, but it's not always a convenient place to live."

She shrugged. "I'll happily run to Logan for big grocery runs if it means I can live here the rest of the time." She tilted her head back just a little so she could catch snowflakes on her tongue.

Nick chuckled. "You're not seeing anyone in Salt Lake?"

Alyssa shook her head. She considered telling him she'd just broken up with someone, but she decided against it. It was good to be completely free of Tim and meet someone who knew nothing about him. "Not at the moment. No girl for you?"

He shook his head. "Foot loose and fancy free." He reached for her hand, taking it with his and pulling her to his side.

She looked up at him warily, wondering exactly what he wanted from her. "That's good," she mumbled.

He turned to her, cupping her face in his hands. He slowly lowered his head, giving her every chance in the world to pull away from him.

Alyssa watched his head slowly descend to hers, and she thought about pulling away, but she felt as if he was a giant magnet and she was a small piece of iron. His kiss was something she'd wanted for what seemed like forever. It might be the biggest mistake of her life, but she would feel like she wasn't really living if she didn't go through with it.

Wrapping her arms around his shoulders, she clung to him for dear life. Her lips parted slightly as he deepened the kiss, and when he pulled away, she felt bereft, missing his touch.

"I . . . I'm not sure I meant for that to happen," she said softly.

"I'm sure I did. It's all I've thought about since the moment I laid eyes on you." Nick smiled, his eyes looking deeply into hers. "And I plan on doing it again the first chance I get."

She bit her lower lip for a moment, wondering if she should let herself get carried away by him. "I don't know if I'm ready to get involved . . ."

"I have news for you, Alyssa. I already feel involved. It's too late to go back to the way things were."

She sighed. "I was afraid of that."

He grinned, and it was a little lopsided, which she hadn't noticed before. Who could keep their heart locked up when it came to Nick and his lopsided grins?

"Go out with me tomorrow night," he said. It wasn't a request either. It was a command.

Alyssa took a deep breath and jumped off the deep end. Why not? She felt so much for him that she couldn't keep hiding away behind her laptop. "All right."

He smiled. "I'm going to leave at six-thirty, shower, and come back for you at seven. Does that work?"

"Am I going to go out with a man with paint in his hair?" she asked, trying to make a joke of it. Tim had always wanted her to be so perfect, but she didn't want that from Nick at all, and he didn't seem to want it from her. She never took special care with her appearance around the house, and he apparently didn't mind. She loved the way he had paint specks in his hair, and he worked so hard. He was someone she could see herself falling completely for. God help her.

"Probably. I mean, I can use turpentine and try to get it out, but I don't know how wise that would be. It would also take a long time . . ."

"I like the paint flecks," she said softly, wondering what she was doing.

"Good. Because I like you, and they seem to be a part of me, whether I want them or not." He took her hand and pulled her back toward the house. "I'd better get back to work, or the boss may fire me."

Alyssa looked up and saw the faces of all three of her sisters pressing against one of the windows upstairs. She did her best to ignore them, knowing what they all must be thinking. She was falling for another man who would control her every move.

But he wouldn't. She wasn't going to let that happen again. Losing herself in a man again was out of the question.

EIGHTEEN

When Alyssa got back into the house, she went upstairs to confront her sisters about their spying. "Did you guys see enough?" she asked, frowning.

Lauren laughed. "We saw that kiss." She waved her hand in front of her face as if she was fanning it. "Looked like a pretty hot one to me. I didn't know we were supposed to be watching you two on all those coffee breaks."

"When did this happen between you two?" Taylor asked. "Why aren't you telling us everything? We want to live vicariously through you!"

Alyssa shook her head, looking at Amanda. "Nothing to add?"

"Well, you have a mint green handprint on your butt, but nothing else." Amanda smirked at her.

Alyssa's face went red. "I do not!"

Amanda pointed to a mirror, and it was then that Alyssa realized her sisters were all in *her room* spying on her. Why that hadn't connected before, she wasn't sure. She walked over to the mirror and turned so she could see her bottom, and her blush got worse. "It's not on my butt. Just my hip."

"Someone's picking nits," Lauren said, shaking her head. "And here we thought you were the serious one, always with your head buried in your studies. It's hard to believe you're the one with a handprint on your bottom."

"Oh, hush up." Alyssa walked to her closet and found a clean pair of jeans, stripping off the paint-covered ones right there as she pulled on the new ones. "Better?"

Taylor smiled. "I'll say. You're putting weight back on, but you've got so much muscle tone, you look amazing."

Alyssa sat down on the edge of her bed and glared at her sisters. "You complain I have paint on my butt, and then you critique my body when I change? There's no doubt you're my sisters."

Amanda walked over and put her arm around Alyssa. "None at all. And there's no doubt we love you beyond measure."

Alyssa rested her head on Amanda's shoulder for a minute. "We're going out tomorrow night. It's my first date with someone other than Tim in like eight years. I don't even remember how to act."

"Not like you acted around Tim. He found it too easy to control you. You have to remember to show some spine." Taylor folded her arms as she looked at her sister. "And you should wear something fun. None of those boring business suits you always wore with Tim."

Alyssa sighed. "All right. I can deal with that."

Amanda got up and went to Alyssa's closet, pulling out different things for Alyssa to potentially wear. "This. I think this is just perfect." She pulled out a skirt that stopped right above the knee and a long-sleeved blouse. "You should wear this with some boots." Amanda kept digging and closed the closet door, frowning. "You don't have any knee-length black boots. What is wrong with you?" She shook her head. "I'll loan you mine." She disappeared from the room, and Alyssa sighed dramatically.

"I feel like you guys are making me your project," Alyssa said. "Am I so desperate I need to be a project?"

Lauren pursed her lips for a moment. "Do you want me to answer that honestly or just smile like I didn't hear the question?"

"Why have enemies when I have sisters?" Alyssa asked just as Amanda came back into the room with a pair of boots in her hand.

Amanda put the footwear at her sister's feet. "Well?"

Alyssa shook her head. "Well, what?"

"Go try the outfit on so we can see how it looks all together."

Alyssa groaned dramatically. "I feel like a Barbie doll you guys are dressing up and trying to change."

"We don't want to change you," Taylor said seriously. "We want to help you make the most of who you already are. No one is ever going to try to change you again on our watch."

Alyssa stood up and walked to Taylor, hugging her tightly. "I do love my sisters."

"And we love you right back. Now try on the clothes!" Lauren said with mock exasperation.

Alyssa quickly stripped and put on the change of clothes Amanda had picked out for her. When she was finished, she did a slow spin for her sisters to see all the angles.

"That's perfect," Taylor said with a smile.

"I get to do your hair!" Amanda said, rubbing her hands together. "You could use a haircut, but I think I can make it work."

Alyssa groaned. "But who's going to do my makeup if you do my hair?" she asked sarcastically.

"Oh, that's totally my job," Lauren said. "I can't wait to get my hands on you." She walked into Alyssa's bathroom and started digging through the drawers there. "Is this all the makeup you have?" She held up a small makeup bag.

"I don't wear much."

"Well, I'm at least using my lipstick on you. It's kiss-proof, and from what I can tell, your lips will be naked halfway through the night if you don't have kiss-proof lipstick on." Lauren shook her head at the meager makeup she found. "Don't tell me . . . Tim didn't think you should wear makeup?"

Alyssa frowned at her sister. "He controlled every little aspect of my life. I lost myself trying to be who he wanted. Please don't ever let me be that stupid again."

"I don't think we'll have to stop you," Taylor said softly. "I think you're too strong to go back to being anyone's puppet."

"Puppet?" Alyssa thought about the word for a moment before she realized just how well it suited what she'd been to Tim. "I guess I was. I'm so glad I dumped him and moved on. And I'm glad you slammed his foot in the door, Taylor. That made for some special memories."

"I just wish I'd done it a little more violently," Taylor said, grinning. "No more talk about Tim. Tell us about that kiss we watched. Did it feel as good as it looked?"

Alyssa smiled, and when she caught a look at her face in the mirror across the room, she realized what a dreamy, happy smile it was. Maybe she was doing the right thing by going out with Nick. He was already making her happier than Tim ever had. "I'm not going to kiss and tell."

"No, but that smile tells us everything," Amanda said with a grin. "Tell him that we all need men just like him."

"I think we all need to focus on the B&B for a while. I shouldn't even be dating the man, but I can't seem to help myself."

Taylor shook her head. "With what you went through with that idiot, you have every right to be happy, and if Nick makes you happy, then I for one am all for it."

"I do think he's going to make me happy," Alyssa said. "And he doesn't seem to want me to become something else. He's happy with me just how I am."

"That's pretty special." Lauren grinned. "I want a man just like him when I grow up."

"Well, if I ever thought that would happen . . ." Alyssa winked at Lauren.

Lauren stuck her tongue out at Alyssa, making her point for her. "Call with Kayla is tonight, right? I hate that we couldn't do it before, but I love that we get to do it now. Do you have your list ready?" Lauren asked Taylor.

"I do. And I have several potential names for the B&B, too. I think once we get these things settled, Amanda can work her magic, and then Kayla and Nick can work their magic, and we'll have a magical B&B." Taylor rubbed her hands together. "I'm so excited, I could just spit."

"Why would excitement be wrapped up with spit?" Lauren asked, looking a bit confused.

"No idea. That was something Hannah and Alyssa used to say all the time. Being here must have brought it back." Taylor shrugged. "Besides, I want to emulate my big sister whenever I can."

"You're all crazy," Alyssa said. "Now, I'm going to change back into my clothes I was wearing before . . . well, the new clothes, and I'm going to soak the paint-on-the-butt jeans, and then I'm going to go back downstairs and do a little more studying. You have all interrupted my day enough."

"We interrupted your day?" Taylor said, looking shocked. "I was working on ideas for the B&B when Lauren called us all in here to watch you and Nick on the beach. My day was interrupted *very* rudely."

Alyssa stood up and changed, deciding to pretend her sisters weren't there. They were all annoying anyway. "Back as you were. There will be no more beach kissing shows today. Well, none starring me anyway." She left her sisters lounging in her room as she headed downstairs to her work. And to Nick, which was so much more important than any studying could ever be.

She sighed. Could Nick really be the man she'd dreamed of her entire life? It sure felt like it.

NINETEEN

ALYSSA and her sisters gathered together around seven to call Kayla. They did a Facetime call from Alyssa's Mac so they could all be part of the call. They put the Mac on the coffee table, and the four of them sat close together on the couch so they were all in the "picture" Kayla would see.

Kayla answered immediately. "Hi! I miss you guys!"

"We miss you, too. It feels like it's been forever since we last saw you."

"Two weeks isn't forever, but it's starting to feel that way." Kayla frowned. "I wish I could get this wrapped up faster, but I found some mold in the basement, and I'm having to pull out all the carpet and redo so much. The basement is finished—or it was before I started ripping it up. I'm going to have to refinish it, so it's going to add weeks if not months to this project."

Alyssa shook her head. "That's awful."

"You have no idea." Kayla rubbed her hands over her eyes. "All right, let's start this business meeting. We're looking at names for the B&B?"

Taylor nodded, picking up her notes. "That's one of the items on the agenda. Let me tell you the names I've come up with, and we'll vote."

"Perfect," Kayla said. She leaned forward eagerly. "It'll be nice to think about something other than my troubles for a minute or two. Our mutual futures sound like a good topic to me."

"Well, I'm going to throw out the four ideas I've come up with, but we can entertain any ideas. We're not limited to these." Taylor glanced at her list. "Lake House B&B. Bear Lake B&B. Richland B&B. Sisters B&B."

Alyssa wrinkled her nose. "The locals call it the Romriell house. Why don't we just use that instead?"

A slow smile spread across Taylor's face. "I love that. Why didn't I think of it?"

Shrugging her shoulders, Alyssa said, "Because you haven't yet learned to think like a local."

Taylor rolled her eyes. "Any other suggestions?"

Amanda shook her head. "Nope. But I'm with Alyssa. I like The Romriell House."

"Me too," Kayla said.

"And me," Lauren responded.

"Well that was easier than I expected it to be," Taylor said. "We'll officially be called The Romriell House. There's a company in Montpelier that we can hire to make our sign." She seemed truly excited to have finished their first task. "I've already set up the corporation. Lauren and I will be drawing a salary bi-monthly. Everyone else will receive quarterly payments. Kayla, if you do work for us, and I know you eventually will, you'll be paid bi-monthly as well. Does that work for everyone?"

There were nods. No one else had really thought about how the money would be split, because none of them were hurting. Well, Lauren didn't have much, but she didn't have any real expenses either.

Lauren leaned toward the monitor. "Just so you know . . . Alyssa is going out with our contractor tomorrow night. He's sexy, and you should have seen their first kiss. I could feel it from the beach." Lauren waved her hand as if fanning her face.

Alyssa shook her head. "Only because you were spying on us."

Kayla laughed. "Lauren, you need to call me tomorrow with all the juicy details. I can't wait to hear, but we're derailing Taylor's meeting, and she scares me when she's in business mode."

Taylor glared at Kayla. "So . . . back on track . . . Amanda thought it would be a good idea to do themes for the rooms, and we've decided to do a book theme for each guest room. I'd like to choose eleven themes. We'll only use seven to start with, but I don't think any of us are planning to live here forever."

There were nods. "Sounds good," Alyssa said. She was excited to hear the list of books her sister had come up with.

"I want us all to vote for our top eleven themes out of the books I have listed. And anyone can feel free to add another, of course. We want to make this fair." Taylor looked at Kayla. "Do you have pen and paper? I think we should all make notes as we go."

Kayla nodded. "I do. Let's do this!"

"Okay, let's just write them all down and number them with your top one through eleven. We can vote from there." Taylor took a deep breath. "And here we go. *A Wrinkle in Time, Hunger Games, Jurassic Park, Princess Bride, Gone with the Wind, Pride and Prejudice, Anne of Green Gables, Heidi, Bridges of Madison County, Harry Potter, Sherlock Holmes, Romeo and Juliet, Scarlet Letter, Huckleberry Finn, Moby Dick, Frankenstein, Flowers for Algernon, The Giver, The Time Machine, Beauty and the Beast, 1984,* and *Hitchhiker's Guide to the Galaxy.*" She spoke slowly and clearly, giving her sisters time to write them all down.

"You forgot *Carrie!*" Alyssa complained. "You know I want a *Carrie* room with blood dripping down the walls."

"Okay, we'll vote on *Carrie* as well." Taylor shook her head as she added *Carrie* to her own list. "Anyone else want to throw something out there?"

Lauren pursed her lips. "How about *In Death?* That series Nora Roberts writes as JD Robb. I think that would be an amazing room."

They all dutifully added *In Death* to their lists.

"Cyrano de Bergerac," Amanda suggested.

When no one else added anything, Taylor said, "Now, number them from your top favorite to number eleven. Amanda can get started on the designs for the top seven immediately."

"Oh, I can? Really?" Amanda asked with just a touch of sarcasm.

"This was *your* idea!" Taylor reminded her.

"And it's a good one," Amanda replied with a smirk.

"Mark your favorites. Quickly, so we don't waste too much of Kayla's time."

"Kayla has nothing more important to do than chat with her favorite sisters." Kayla grinned, looking down at her list.

It took them all less than five minutes to finish, and Taylor ran down the list again, asking if anyone had voted for each individual book in their top seven.

When they had all finished with the voting, Taylor sighed. "Well that was fun. Here's our list. The first seven to be done are: *Harry Potter,* of course, *Hunger Games, Beauty and the Beast, Princess Bride, Moby Dick, Anne of Green Gables,* and *Pride and Prejudice.* Then our four runners up, which will be done as the house gets emptier with sisters and fuller with guests, are *Jurassic Park, Frankenstein, Huck Finn,* and *Heidi.*" She looked over at Amanda. "I'll give you my list in the order I want the rooms done tomorrow, so you can get started."

"No *Carrie?*" Alyssa said, trying to sound mortified.

"You were the only one who even thought *Carrie* should have the possibility of getting a vote. No *Carrie.* No blood running down the walls of one of the guest rooms. Sorry to disappoint you, Alyssa." Amanda shook her head.

"Fine." Alyssa grinned. She wouldn't have been able to walk in the room if they'd done it anyway, and she was sure she was going to be asked to help keep things clean at least while she lived there.

Kayla smiled. "Is that all our business for the day?"

"Yup. That's it. We've covered everything we need to cover."

"Good. I was thinking of driving up next weekend, but with the flooding in the basement, I'm going to have to resist for now." Kayla shook her head. "I want to see my treehouse!"

Taylor opened her eyes wide. "I forgot! There is something else I want to discuss while we're all here."

"Go for it," Kayla said.

"I was thinking we might want to spruce up the treehouse and maybe build some playground equipment. A volleyball court wouldn't go amiss. And when everything else is done, maybe an outdoor kitchen. This is the perfect place for cookouts, and since I plan on a mini-fridge in every room, that could be a free service we offer the guests. They'd have to sign up in advance so every single guest isn't trying to use it at the same time, but it really would be nice."

Alyssa nodded. "I think that would be smart. We certainly have enough land for it."

"Are we sharing the hot tub and sauna with guests?" Lauren asked.

"I hadn't thought of that," Taylor said. "Probably, though. I think it would be a selling point."

"We're going to want to make sure it's drained and cleaned more often, then," Alyssa said. "That will be a little extra work."

"Extra work for the girl with a liberal arts degree?" Lauren asked. "I really don't know what else to do with that piece of useless paper."

They all laughed. "You know, you have a degree, and that's pretty awesome," Kayla said. "I don't."

Alyssa shook her head. "You guys are a mess. Taylor, I think the ideas for the outdoor kitchen and the playground are wonderful. It will bring in families as clientele, and I think we all want others to have the same special memories of this home as we do."

They chatted for another hour about nothing and everything.

Finally, Kayla yawned. "I was up at five ripping out the flooring in the basement, and I have a lot of long days ahead of me. I'm going to hang up now and take a long hot shower for my aching muscles, and then fall into my bed and sleep like the dead until about five tomorrow morning."

Alyssa glanced at the clock on her laptop and saw that it was after nine. "Sounds good to me. I want to get a little more study time in before bed anyway."

"Are Idaho laws so different than Utah?" Lauren asked right after the call ended.

"I just need to make sure I know them cold. You know what an overachiever I am. I accept nothing less than perfection." Alyssa hated to admit it, but she was pretty darn crazy about doing everything to the very best of her ability. It was both a strength and a weakness.

"I do," Lauren said. "That's why I worry about you sometimes. You try so hard and obsess about doing everything just right. I'd be happy to make a passing grade. You won't be any more licensed with that higher score."

"I know." Alyssa shrugged. "Maybe I'll get past it someday, but for now, it serves me well."

"It does." Lauren got to her feet. "Well, goodnight. I'm going to sleep like the dead."

Amanda and Taylor both got up to leave as well.

"We're going to work in the dining room on some of the room ideas," Taylor said.

"Sounds good." Alyssa already had her study program up and was working on a practice test. They'd accomplished the family business, and now it was time for her personal business.

TWENTY

When Nick arrived at work on Saturday, he was feeling a little self-conscious. He wasn't sure Alyssa had noticed, but all three of her sisters had been in an upstairs bedroom watching them when they'd come back from the beach. It wasn't that he wanted to hide their relationship, but it was strange that they'd been all looking on the way they had.

He got to work painting straight away, not paying any attention to the comings and goings of the sisters around him. He'd gotten used to their chatter after almost two weeks of working there. It was past eight when Alyssa walked into the kitchen.

"There are donuts on the dining room table, and there's more than enough to share," she said softly. "But I have a bone to pick with you first."

He frowned at her, wondering what on earth she was upset about. He hadn't talked to her since the afternoon before, and she'd been perfectly fine with him then. His gaze dropped to her lips, and he briefly considered pulling her to him for a kiss, but her annoyed look put that idea to rest. "What did I do?"

"You put a mint green handprint on the butt of one of my most comfortable pairs of jeans."

He smirked, shaking his head. "Oh, did I?" He'd realized it the day before, but he could just imagine the look on her face if he'd told her, so he'd kept that little piece of information to himself. "You knew you did!" She glared at him. "You could have told me! One of my sisters pointed it out, and they all laughed at me."

"Isn't that what sisters are supposed to do?" he asked. He wasn't even a little bit repentant. He'd branded her as his in the only way he knew how. The fact that it hadn't been deliberate was beside the point.

"I'd really rather they didn't!" She shook her head at him. "I can't believe you didn't say something."

"I wasn't sure how you'd react," he said honestly. "Besides, it will make for great memories of our first kiss."

Her eyes grew wide, and she stepped back a little. "Why do we need memories? It's easy enough to do it again if we want."

"Anytime we want. Now sounds good, doesn't it?" He looked in every direction before catching her hand, pulling her toward him, lowering his head, and kissing her softly. "Good morning."

"Don't think you're going to get past me with your sweet talk and even sweeter kisses. You're still in trouble."

"You think my kisses are sweet? I can change that at any time you'd like . . ."

She laughed just a little. "You, Nick Peot, are incorrigible."

"And you, Alyssa Romriell, are beautiful. I can't believe I made it through thirty-two years of life without you in it." He kissed her once more and raised his head when he heard applause. All three of her sisters were standing there watching them.

"That's the way to kiss her," Lauren said, cheering him on.

"I have a feeling we're going to have to do any romancing we want to do away from the house," he said, shaking his head at them. "Do you not understand that your sister needs a little bit of privacy while a man kisses her socks off?"

"Oh, pardon us." Amanda put her arms around Lauren and Taylor. "We'll just go eat our donuts, and leave you two to it. Carry on." She turned them all around, and they walked like a six-legged monster toward the dining room.

Alyssa's face was flaming red. "Is sororicide illegal in this country? If it is, I might have to get a law degree just so I can fight the law."

He laughed. "You love your sisters too much for that." He sighed. "Let's go get some donuts before your sisters eat them all."

"I get the lemon filled." Alyssa said, heading into the dining room ahead of him. "You can have whatever the vultures leave for you."

Taylor gasped. "Did you really just call your *favorite sisters* vultures?"

"At the moment, *Kayla* is my favorite sister," Alyssa said, reaching for her lemon-filled donuts.

"That's understandable," Lauren said. "I mean, we did interrupt a make-out session in the kitchen. An entirely inappropriate make-out session, I might add. That's not what we hired Nick to do!"

Alyssa sat down amidst the teasing and sighed. "I forgot to get my coffee." They had plugged the coffee maker into an outlet in the dining room, so they wouldn't miss out on their daily dose of caffeine. She got up and poured herself a mug, looking around. "Anyone else need a shot?"

Nick held up his own mug, and her sisters all already had drinks. He watched as she sat back down, directly across from him. He liked her there, because he could look at her to his heart's content. "So, I should have the painting finished today, and then I'll start laying the floor. Cabinets will go in tomorrow or Monday." He was getting fatigued by the seven-day work weeks, but he'd definitely worked them into his quote, and he wasn't going to complain even a little bit.

"So, I'll be able to start cooking again tomorrow?" Lauren asked.

"Nope. Appliances won't go in until Tuesday or Wednesday probably. I'll do everything I can to get all the tile laid today." He rubbed the back of his neck. "But I'm leaving thirty minutes early this evening. I have a hot date."

Alyssa turned red yet again, and he loved it. The woman could blush like no one he'd seen since high school. "No comment."

All of the sisters laughed, and he grinned. "She *is* fun to tease, isn't she?"

"More fun than any of the rest of us, that's for sure," Amanda said. "She is the only person I know who blushes quite that easily or that red. It's pure joy to watch."

"I have to agree with that. Although, I'd be happy watching her all day even if she wasn't blushing." He watched her and noticed her color deepening. "I do think we should lay off, though. I mean, her extremities need blood, and it's apparently all in her face."

Alyssa finished her donut and got to her feet. "I'm going for my run." She walked toward the door, wearing a pair of leggings and an oversized shirt. He loved seeing her legs with the skin-tight pants. She was the most beautiful and real woman he'd ever known. There were no complaints on his part.

After the door closed, he felt the eyes of every sister on him.

"You will *not* hurt her," Lauren said softly. "She's fragile, and she's had enough ridiculously controlling men in her life. You will not be another."

Amanda's eyes narrowed at him. "We like you, Nick, but we will do everything we can to make your life a living hell if you cause her to shed even one tear."

Taylor nodded, letting him know the threat was from her as well.

"I don't intend to hurt her. She's way too special for that." Nick frowned. "I guess you all gang up on every man who is interested in her?"

Taylor's eyes looked bleak. "If only we had. We're trying to rectify past mistakes."

Nick had no idea what it was that had them all so upset and protective of their older sister, but he would be extra careful with her feelings. He had no desire to hurt her, but more than that, he had no desire to let her get away. He wanted a lifetime with her in a way he'd never wanted with anyone else. He'd proposed to Kami because she'd pressured him a lot, finally telling him she was going to dump him if he didn't. He shouldn't have given into the pressure, but he hadn't expected to find anyone quite like Alyssa.

"I'm going to get back to work. I promise I will do everything in my power not to hurt her. She's going to feel loved and cherished on my watch." He left the three sisters sitting at the table, returning to his job. His mind was on everything they'd said.

He wished they'd met ten years before. It would have saved them both a lot of heartache. If she'd been hurt so badly, it did explain how skittish she'd been. Picking up his paint roller, he lost himself in his work, but he couldn't stop thinking about Alyssa and wondering what exactly had happened to make her younger sisters so terribly protective of her.

TWENTY-ONE

ALYSSA RAN on the beach that morning because it had finally stopped snowing, if only for a day. She knew there was a great deal more snow in the forecast, but the sun was shining, and the birds were singing, and she was going to take advantage of it.

As she ran, her mind flowed from topic to topic, and she had to wonder what was wrong with her sisters to always feel the need to make her blush. She was both apprehensive and excited about her first date with Nick, and she knew her sisters would milk her embarrassment for all it was worth.

When she had finished her run, she studied a good portion of the day, sitting in the living room.

It was shortly past noon when Nick came to the doorway, looking at her. "I thought you might want to see how the floor is coming."

She set her computer down and walked with him to the kitchen, smiling when she saw how good the tile looked. She was glad to see the brown-patterned linoleum gone and the pretty tiles taking its place. "It's starting to look really good!"

"Just wait until all the new stainless-steel appliances and the cupboards are in. This kitchen is going to be a showpiece."

"I can't wait. I want it to be done now!"

He grinned. "So, what books did you ladies decide on in your meeting last night? You did have it last night, didn't you?"

She nodded. "We decided on a bunch. I think the first one that you'll be working on is *Anne of Green Gables*."

"I'm not painting a mural on the wall or anything, am I?"

"I don't think so. If we need something like that, I'm sure we'll call in an artist. We have an aunt who used to summer here with us. She is absolutely incredible. Hopefully if it comes to that, she'll be willing to do a mural. I honestly am not sure what Amanda and Taylor have in mind for things like that. I guess I should ask, but I trust them both, so I'm not overly concerned about it."

"Makes sense." He reached down and caught her hand with his, giving it a good squeeze. "Go back and study, and I'll work. I'm excited about spending some time with you tonight."

She smiled nervously. "Me too." Standing on tiptoe, she pressed her lips to his cheek, feeling very brave as she did so. Tim had hated her spontaneous shows of affection and had verbally beaten them out of her.

"Feel free to do that anytime," he said, wiggling his eyebrows at her.

She was surprised at how good his words made her feel, almost completely blocking Tim's voice out of her head for the moment. "Okay, back to studying."

"Back to laying tile."

It was hard to walk away from him, and that surprised her. She'd always been mildly relieved when she no longer had to spend time with Tim, but she'd wanted more time with him anyway. She was sure she'd been demented for the seven years they were together. There was no other explanation.

It was just after five when Amanda came downstairs. "Time to get ready."

Alyssa frowned. "I have two hours."

"And we're going to take every minute of that time," Amanda assured her. "Up you go. Shower and wash your hair. I'll be waiting."

"Fine." Alyssa stomped up the stairs grudgingly. It wasn't as if she'd never gotten herself ready for a date. She was perfectly capable of doing this with no help from her sisters. She truly wasn't sure what their problems were.

She took a long, hot shower, refusing to be rushed. When she was finished, she walked into her bedroom and was surprised at the fact that all three of her sisters were there. "Et tu, Taylor?"

"I'm just here to watch the show." Taylor grinned at her happily.

"Great. Maybe if you guys film it, you'll get some kind of award for the biggest transformation in the history of women."

"I think that went to Eliza Doolittle." Lauren looked at her for a moment. "We're starting with a facial. I know you don't want it, but I really don't care at the moment." She walked to her sister and put some sort of gross cream on her face, slathering it everywhere. It took her more than five minutes to cover Alyssa's face in just the way she wanted. "I have a little goop left. Sit up, Taylor." Taylor had been lounging on Alyssa's bed as if she owned the place.

Taylor shrugged and sat up. "I can use all the beauty treatments you want to give me."

Lauren didn't respond to that nonsense as she smeared the cream on Taylor's face.

While Alyssa watched the whole process, she was aware that Amanda was messing with her hair. She may not look like herself that evening, but that would be a good thing, right?

Her sisters chattered around her as she sat and allowed them to pull and prod her for the next hour and a half. Finally, her mask was off, and her hair was finished.

"Don't look in the mirror until you're dressed and your makeup is on," Lauren said, waiting as her sister changed into the clothes they'd picked out for her night out with Nick. "Now sit again, and I'll fix your makeup."

Alyssa sighed. "You guys aren't going to do this every time I have a date, are you?"

"Nope. We're going to teach you to do it," Lauren said. She looked like an artist with her palette as she held all the colors of eyeshadow she was using in one hand and a small makeup brush in the other. "Blink."

They barely had her ready in time. It was five minutes before seven when they finally let Alyssa look in the mirror, and she felt as if she was seeing someone else. Her lips were a much brighter shade of red than she would have put on herself, and her eyes were painted darkly. "I think it's too much makeup!"

Taylor shook her head. "No, it's just the right amount. You look even more beautiful than usual, Alyssa. Don't you *dare* wash your face."

Alyssa sighed, turning her head to one side as she looked at how her hair had been done. It curled softly around her face. "I won't wash my face." She picked up her purse. "I need to go down and wait for him."

"Oh, no you don't. You do not need to look overly eager. Make an entrance," Lauren said.

"I draw the line at making an entrance. Making him wait would be rude, and that's just not who I am." Alyssa walked down the stairs, and the doorbell rang just as she got to the bottom. She walked over and opened the door, smiling at him. "Let me just get my coat."

Nick grinned, grabbing her hand. "Get your coat, but first let me tell you something."

She looked up at him. "What's that?"

"I think you always look beautiful, but tonight, you've knocked my socks off." With those words, he let her go, and she hurried away for her coat.

It took her a minute to calm her breath after his comment. How was she going to make it if it didn't work out between them? Her heart hadn't been broken when she and Tim had ended things. In fact, she'd been more relieved than anything else. With Nick, she knew it would be different. He was going to really hurt her if they couldn't make things work.

When she got to the door, he helped her put her coat on, and she looked back to see all three of her sisters watching them. They were ridiculous. "Go away!"

Taylor smiled. "Don't stay out too late. You need to be able to study tomorrow."

"Don't do anything I wouldn't do!" Lauren added.

Amanda just stood there grinning at them, looking like a lunatic. Why she loved her sisters was beyond her at that moment. All she wanted to do was get away from them and be alone with Nick.

"Let's get out of here," she said.

"Don't keep her out too late!" Taylor said to Nick. Alyssa was sure she was moving onto Nick because she hadn't been able to get a rise out of her. Whatever. She just needed to be away.

"Ignore them," Alyssa hissed under her breath.

"I'll take good care of her," Nick told them.

"Drive carefully," Amanda said as they closed the door behind them.

Alyssa shook her head. "All but that last thing was a joke. We're always a little worried when one of us goes out after dark now."

"Why is that?"

She looked at him with surprise. "You know our parents were killed in a car wreck in March, don't you?"

"No! I'm so sorry."

Alyssa shook her head. "Why did you think we were taking over the house?"

"I guess I never really thought about it." He took her hand in his and squeezed it. "I'll be extra careful."

TWENTY-TWO

Nick couldn't believe he'd talked Alyssa into going out with him. She seemed a little too . . . well, a little too classy for him, but he was happy to spend time with her. He took her to a local restaurant. It wasn't the nicest one in town, but it was the nicest that wouldn't have a problem with him having paint in his hair, and the green just wasn't coming out.

He'd at least washed up, and he wore a pair of slacks and a collared shirt, realizing that though Kami had wanted him to dress nicer, and he'd refused, now he was dressing up for Alyssa without being asked. He wanted to please Alyssa in a way he'd never cared if he pleased Kami.

When he walked into Hank's Bar and Grill, he felt every eye in the place on him. He'd lived there for too long for him to get by with bringing in a new girl without everyone saying something.

Hank's place was very much a country restaurant. The place was wooden and looked very homey to him, and he always felt good there. There was music blaring from karaoke night in the corner, and people seemed excited as they sang along. No one was really dancing yet, but that usually happened on karaoke night. He wished he'd chosen a quieter place, but they would make it work.

A short blonde who he'd known for years came over to seat them. "Hey, Nick. How's it going?"

"Good. How 'bout with you?"

"I'm expecting again, and I'm sick all the time, so you really don't want to ask me that." She picked up two menus and led them around the tables to a quiet corner of the place. Well, as quiet as a local hangout could be on a Saturday night. "Stacy is going to be your server tonight."

"Sounds good. Hope you feel better."

Alyssa looked at him curiously. "I take it you know her?"

He looked over at the retreating blonde. "Jennifer? Sure. I've known her forever, like everyone else in town."

She smiled, shaking her head. "It surprises me just how small this town is."

"It's home," he said softly.

"Yes, it is."

He looked up and saw Ryan headed straight for them, a soft drink in his hand. "Hey, man."

Ryan raised an eyebrow. "Hello. And who is this lovely lady?"

"This is Alyssa Romriell. She's been a summer person her whole life, and she and her sisters are turning their family's vacation house into a B&B." Nick wanted to hide her away from the prying eyes of his friend, but he knew that wasn't wise.

Ryan looked at her curiously. "Now, I can't imagine you being with Nick willingly. I want you to blink three times if you need help. If you want to be rescued by a gallant gentleman without green paint in his hair, I'm your man."

Alyssa smiled at that. "I really did agree to go out with him."

Nick shook his head. "This joker is my best friend, Ryan. We've been inseparable since we were both in diapers."

"It's nice to meet you," she said softly.

"Now go away," Nick told his friend.

Instead, Ryan snagged a chair from another table and sat in it backward, taking a drink from his pop. "He doesn't mean it," he told Alyssa. "He loves me like a brother."

Nick said nothing, just leveling a stare at his friend. "I do love you like a brother, but I'd love you a lot more if you were across the room."

"See how he treats me?" Ryan said, shaking his head sadly. "I don't know how we've stayed friends all these years. I should have found a new best friend by now, don't you think?"

"No one else would have you, and you know it as well as I do." Nick looked up as the waitress approached. "Hey, Stacy."

"Hiya, Nick. Good to see you out and about." Stacy looked at Alyssa curiously. "You here with him on purpose?"

Alyssa laughed. "You're the second person to ask me that. I promise I do not need to be rescued, and we don't need to have a secret signal like me blinking three times rapidly so you know to get me out of here."

"All right. If you say so." Stacy grinned at her before turning to Nick. "What can I get you? Other than a tow truck for this reprobate, who should not be horning in on your time with the lady."

Nick glanced over at Alyssa. "We haven't had a chance to look at the menu yet, but I'll take a Dr. Pepper, and if I know the lady at all, she'll have a Coke."

Stacy looked at Alyssa. "Does he know you?"

"He does. But he doesn't know that I drink Shirley Temples everywhere I think will have cherries and grenadine." Alyssa shrugged, looking at Nick. "Sorry, but I had to follow my taste buds and not let you be right."

He sighed. "I'm never right."

Stacy laughed and hurried away.

Ryan had to pick up the conversational gambit. "I have to agree with Nick. He is really and truly never right. If you don't mind that, though, you two will probably get along fine."

Alyssa shook her head. "I'm glad Hannah is more supportive of me than you are of Nick."

"Hannah?" Ryan asked. "Not Hannah Baldwin?"

"Yes, do you know her?" She laughed softly. "Why do I even ask? Everyone here knows everyone else."

Ryan shrugged. "Sure, I know Hannah. I've known her all my life."

"I have, too," Alyssa said. "We met the summer before we both started kindergarten."

"Hannah is the one who told me about the job at the Romriell house, and she's the reason I have it. I'm not sure Alyssa would have taken a chance on me otherwise." Nick reached for the drink Stacy set in front of him, taking a sip. "Now, Ryan, if you'll go away, the lady and I can decide what we're having for our dinner."

Ryan frowned. "You want me to eat alone?"

"You're not here alone any more than I am. You're either here with a girl or here with a buddy."

"I'm here with Billy Johnson from Georgetown. He wanted to drink and needed a designated driver, and he always calls me. He knows I won't let anyone be on the roads drinking if I can help it."

"But you left him alone?"

Ryan rolled his eyes. "He's flirting with a barstool and calling her Sally. He's totally wasted. We already ate, and now he's on to the antic portion of his evening." He stood up, smiling at Alyssa. "I'm glad I got to meet you. Welcome to living on the lake full time."

"Very nice to meet you," Alyssa returned. "You can always tell something about a man by the way he treats his friends."

Ryan laughed. "Now don't go dumping Nick for the way he treated me there . . . I was infringing on your date."

"This is our first date, so there would be no dumping. It would simply be a refusal to go out again."

"Well, don't do that either!" Ryan lifted his glass in a salute, backing away from the table. When he was completely behind Alyssa, he caught Nick's eye, giving him a thumbs up.

Nick ignored his friend and opened his menu. "They have great fried cheese curds here. The burgers are to die for."

Alyssa smiled, opening her own menu. "Let me see what catches my eye, and I'll ask if it's any good."

"The only thing I don't like is their country-fried steak. It's no good."

"I'll keep that in mind." He watched her as she perused the menu, glad that they were finally alone—well, as alone as they could be in a room full of people. "I think I'm going to go with a bacon cheeseburger. How are the fries?"

"It's Idaho. All the potatoes are fabulous," he said, winking at her.

She laughed. "I've heard that somewhere before."

"Do you want to split a fried cheese curd to start off with?"

"I'd love to." She took another sip of her Shirley Temple before pushing it to the edge of the table.

"You already need another?"

"My body wants all the sugar it can get its taste buds on."

He reached over and took her hand in his, not caring that everyone in the bar was watching them. "I can understand that." He frowned at her. "Tell me about your parents."

She shook her head. "I'm not sure I'm ready to talk about that just yet. The loss is too recent. Why don't you tell me about Ryan?"

Nick smiled. "He really is like a brother to me. Our moms were friends all through school and they were pregnant at the same time. We were expected to be best friends, and we were. His parents were killed by drunk drivers when we were in high school, and he moved in with my family. My parents already saw him as another son, so it worked out perfectly."

"I can see that." Alyssa smiled, squeezing Nick's hand. "Sounds like your parents are pretty amazing people."

"They are. I wouldn't trade them for anything."

TWENTY-THREE

After her real estate exam in Pocatello a couple of weeks later, Alyssa made the long drive back to Richland. She'd received texts from all of her sisters and from Nick asking how she'd done on the test, but she'd stayed radio silent, wanting to tell them in person.

She loved this drive and the beauty of the area, though it was snowing as she made her way home. Why it was snowing again in mid-May was beyond her, but she really did hope it was almost done for the year. The snow felt better in Idaho than it ever had in Utah, but enough was enough.

Walking into the house, the first person she saw was Nick, who was building a counter and a place to hang keys in the entryway. She didn't meet his gaze and walked straight to the intercom. "I need to see everyone in the kitchen please."

Then she went to the kitchen and pulled out the things she needed to make a sandwich. She'd been so excited to tell everyone that she hadn't wanted to stop and eat, and now she was famished. Maybe she'd have *two* sandwiches.

Nick joined her in the kitchen, looking at her with a raised eyebrow. "You wanna tell me how it went?"

She shook her head, still avoiding eye contact. She was sure he'd be able to look into her eyes and see that she had passed. She wanted to tell everyone all at once.

Within a minute, all of her sisters—except Kayla, who had found another leak in the house she was working on—were in the kitchen with her. She finished her sandwich and looked up, and she knew her grin was completely covering her face. "A perfect score."

Lauren laughed and walked over to hug her. "You and your perfectionism . . ."

Nick waited until her sisters had all congratulated her before moving in on her. He wrapped his arms around her and lifted her off her feet, spinning her in a circle. "You amaze me a little more every day, Alyssa."

Alyssa grinned up at him, wondering how she'd gotten so lucky to have a man like him interested in her. She felt like she was walking on air half the time. "I'm just glad it's over, and I can move onto finding an office. You know of any place?" she asked Nick. He had so many more connections in the area than she did that it only made sense to ask him. If something was available, he would know about it.

"I think I do. . . . Do you care if your office is on this side of the Utah border or the other?"

"Not at all. I just care that I don't have to drive more than thirty minutes."

Nick nodded. "I know just the place, then. We'll go see it tomorrow."

"Tomorrow? What about the entryway?" Alyssa felt herself getting excited to have some time to do something with him during the day, but she didn't want to monopolize him when there was so much work to be done.

"I'll have that finished today."

Amanda frowned at him. "What about the bedrooms?"

He sighed. "I've worked four weeks without a single day off. How about letting me spend a day with the most beautiful woman I know?"

Taylor nodded. "You deserve a day off. Sorry we've worked you so hard." She glanced at her phone. "Tomorrow's Friday. Take off until Monday, and then start on the bedrooms. If they're not all done by the first, life will go on."

"I'm not going to do that. I know how important this is to you ladies. I think I can do my part in a bed and bath in about three days. We want as many of them fully functional as we can make happen."

"That's true," Taylor said with a nod. "And since we're all here . . . we got our first reservation today!"

Lauren squealed, hugging Taylor. "Wow! Two things to celebrate. Well, three if we include the entryway being done. It's like everything is falling into place."

Amanda nodded. "I'm thrilled. And I may go with you two to see that office. Maybe we could divide one in half, and I could work out of it, too."

Alyssa shrugged. "That's fine with me if Nick doesn't mind."

"Oh, sure. I don't care. I was going to take you out for a nice lunch, but I guess we can all go." He didn't sound terribly thrilled about taking Amanda along, and she understood, because she wanted to be alone with him, too. But it made sense for the two sisters to see it together.

"Sounds good to me." Alyssa grinned. "I can't wait to start working again. I feel like I've been sitting around *way* too much lately."

"We all have," Taylor said. "I'm ready for this place to be up and running." She looked at Nick. "How much of the time you have allotted for doing the rooms and bedrooms will be devoted to cleaning up when you're done?"

He shrugged. "Couple of hours each, probably."

Lauren clapped her hands. "I can do that! It'll give me something to do other than practice making breakfasts!"

"Well, that'll help, then." Nick grinned. "We're going to be ready on time. I promise you that, ladies." He wrapped his arm around Alyssa's shoulders. "But I want a fifteen-minute walk on the beach with this sweet girl before I finish the entryway. Anyone care?"

Amanda shook her head. "You two go and have fun. Take *twenty* minutes if you want."

Alyssa laughed. "You're *so* generous." She walked to the fridge and got two bottles of water, handing Nick one. "We'll be back soon."

They both had to put on winter coats to go outside, despite the fact that it was mid-May. Finally, he opened the door and led her outside. "I love the smell of new-fallen snow."

"Me too. I love that you can smell the snow here and not *just* the pollution." Hand-in-hand, they walked toward the water. There was no standing snow, even though it was falling from the sky. "I hope it's not cold enough for the snow to accumulate. I'm kind of done with it."

He laughed. "You can be done all you want, but I'm not sure it's over yet." He pulled her closer to him, wrapping an arm around her waist as they walked. "I'm really proud of you for doing so well on your test."

She rested her head against his shoulder for a minute. Tim would have found something she should have done differently. Probably complained that she took time from him by studying so hard when a seventy would have been good enough. She was so glad Nick was different. "Thank you. I'm really excited about starting a business here."

"You should be." He kissed the top of her head. "And if anyone needs a contractor . . ."

She laughed. "Yes, I will recommend you. But I would have anyway."

"I know that."

They reached the edge of the lake, and turned to walk along it. "Is the office you saw in Garden City?"

He nodded. "There are actually two in that same building, and from what I understand, both are kind of small. You and Amanda may want to each get one."

"We probably will. I'm not one to spend much time in the office, but we'll see. I do need space for files and all that good stuff."

"So now that you're done studying, do you have any big plans?"

She shrugged. "I need to go to Utah on Monday. I have a client who thinks she found the house she wants, but I need to show it to her. I'll probably spend the night with Kayla."

"Oh. I didn't realize you'd still be working with people in Utah."

"Not often. This one is special. I sold her the house she owns now, and she's ready to upgrade. She doesn't want to work with anyone else, so it's got to be me, apparently."

"That actually makes a lot of sense," he said. "I would probably feel the same."

"Have you ever thought about buying a house and fixing it up to be an Airbnb or even flipping? I could see you doing really well at that."

He shrugged. "I've thought of it. I don't want to have to deal with the Airbnb, though. Sounds like it would be a pain in my butt."

She laughed softly. "Well, maybe it would." She stopped walking and looked at him. "Do you realize I don't even know where you live?"

He chuckled. "A cabin in the woods between here and Fish Haven. I built it myself between jobs. It's pretty special to me."

"Well, I'd love to see it someday."

He leaned down and brushed his lips against hers. "I guess we can make that happen. You just let me know when you're free."

She pursed her lips. "Maybe I could cook you supper there tomorrow, since you're off work."

"I think that would be amazing. We'll dump your sister after lunch, and I'll take you back to my place. I love the idea of just sitting around with you and spending time together. Or we could catch a movie if you'd prefer."

"Why don't we rent a movie from Amazon, so we can be alone?" They had never truly been alone. Their walks on the beach didn't count, because she never knew if she had a sister or three watching from one of the windows.

"That sounds like the perfect solution to me!"

As they headed back toward the house, she tried to decide what to cook the following night. Whatever it was, she needed to wow him. She wanted him to keep her around.

TWENTY-FOUR

When Nick went to pick up the two sisters the following morning, Alyssa insisted they take her SUV because it would be easier for them all to fit than in his pickup, and he held his hand out for the keys.

She frowned at him. "Are you kidding me? You don't trust me to drive?"

"Sure, I do. I just know where we're going, and it'll be easier than trying to give you directions." He preferred to be in control when it came to vehicles, and he always had. He didn't want to tell her that, though. It would probably be best if she didn't figure it out until they'd been married ten or twenty years.

She sighed, putting her keys in his hand. "Fine." She got into the passenger side while Amanda got into the back. "What are we doing for lunch?"

He shrugged. "I don't really know. I just figured we'd go somewhere."

Amanda leaned forward. "That's what I like. A man with a plan."

"We'll eat. I'm hoping my favorite burger place is open for the season, but if not, there's a great little place in Garden City where we can go." Nick looked at Amanda in the rearview mirror for a fraction of a second as he spoke.

"Do you have any idea when the crepe place opens?" Alyssa asked. "I remember going there every summer, and I might start going there every day once I start working out of the office." He could hear the excitement in her voice as she talked about them.

He laughed. "I think they open the weekend of Memorial Day like everything else, but I'm not sure."

When they reached the building the offices were in, Nick took Alyssa's hand. "I hope you like this place. I think it's just perfect."

There was a commercial real estate agent waiting for them at the door. "Who's the office for?" she asked.

"My sister and I are both looking for offices. I'm a real estate agent, and she's an interior designer."

"I see. Well, let me show you what I have available. I'm Margo, by the way."

"I'm Alyssa, and my sister is Amanda."

They followed Margo into the building, and down a hallway.

"I have two offices, and either would work." Margo opened a door to the first one. It was extremely small, but it was all Alyssa would need. She walked in, smelling deeply of the room. She'd learned that she couldn't deal with musty smells very well, but the office smelled clean.

"This would probably work for me." Alyssa opened a door and found a bathroom. "Does this connect to the other available office?" she asked.

"Yes, it does. Let's just go through here." Opening the door, Margo showed them a second office that was just a touch bigger.

Amanda walked in and spun around. "This one would work better for me, but I'm not sure we could share like we talked about." She went to the window and looked out. "These are small."

"I agree," Alyssa said. "How much?"

The agent named a price that Alyssa was surprised by. "That's extremely reasonable. I want the smaller office, I think."

Amanda smiled. "And I'll take the bigger one."

"Well, you two are easy to get along with, aren't you?" Margo pulled a folder from under her arm and opened it. "I brought the paperwork. A twelve-month lease is required, and the owner does want a deposit." Margo went on to explain all the details, and the sisters grinned at each other.

"I'm glad we're going to be work neighbors." Alyssa said. "It'll be really nice when we're not living together anymore."

"Yeah. I agree. Not sure how much longer I'm going to survive with a communal kitchen."

Alyssa laughed softly. "We're only a month into this thing . . ."

"I know. Whatever. I'm getting a dorm fridge for my office, I think. And a microwave. Is there a shared kitchen here, too?" Amanda asked Margo.

"No, there's not. Most people have a microwave and fridge. Now, I do need you to know that hot plates aren't allowed."

"That makes sense to me." Alyssa signed her name on the line indicated by Margo.

Thirty minutes later, they left the building.

"Now, food!" Amanda said. "I'm hungry."

"My burger place isn't open yet, but I'll take you to that place I like near here." Nick got into the car and waited for the sisters to do the same. "What are you making me for supper tonight?"

Alyssa smiled. "I'm making fajitas. How does that sound?"

"Good to me," Nick said. "I can't believe I haven't even shown you my house yet. I'm awfully proud of it, and I usually show it off pretty darn quick."

"Well, you have been at my house every day and working ridiculously long hours. It makes sense."

"Yeah, it does." He watched her for a moment, smiling. "I'm excited to show it off to you tonight."

Amanda sighed. “I’ll just sit back here and pretend someone is talking to me.”

“Play on your phone!” Alyssa said.

Nick grinned. “We’ll try to include you. Sorry for that.”

“No big deal. I have a phone.”

TWENTY-FIVE

AFTER LUNCH, Nick dropped Amanda off at the house, and then he and Alyssa went to the grocery store. He insisted on buying the ingredients for the meal.

"Is this the grocery store where Hannah worked?" she asked.

"Yup. She worked here for years. I'm surprised you didn't come see her while she worked here."

Alyssa sighed. "After high school, I did the college thing, majoring in marketing. I was so busy every weekend that I never made it back with my parents. I did summer school every year and just threw myself into being a perfectionist like I'd always been."

"You've always worked this hard?" he asked, a little surprised.

"Our parents instilled a strong work ethic in all of us. I was valedictorian of my high school class and graduated *summa cum laude* from my college. And I immediately started my real estate classes when I was done. I never took the time to come back to the lake, because I was too busy adulting. I regret that now."

"So even after you started selling real estate you never took a weekend off?" Nick had thought he was a hard worker until he'd met Alyssa.

"Very rarely. There were always people who needed to see houses on the weekends. Saturdays have always been my biggest sales day." She shrugged. "And I started seeing someone, and he took up a lot of my time, too." It was the first time she'd mentioned Tim to him, and she wasn't sure how much she wanted to tell him, but he had to know he wasn't the first man she'd dated.

"Oh?"

She nodded, putting grated cheese into her cart. "Yup. I just got out of a seven-year relationship in March. Best thing I've ever done for myself."

He didn't ask anything else, and she didn't volunteer more. They checked out, and then he drove the short distance to the cabin.

Heading up the long driveway, he grinned. "So, I usually start planting around the first of June. I like to have flower beds along each side of the driveway."

"Are you going to have time for that this year?" she asked.

"I have no idea. I sure hope so. I might have to hire someone to do the lawn and maybe do some planting."

"Makes sense to me," Alyssa said. "We've never mentioned your parents really. Are they still in the area?"

He shook his head. "Nah, they moved somewhere warmer a couple of years back. Got tired of the cold. I really need to go visit them in Tucson."

"I can understand that." She got out and walked around to the back to help carry in the groceries. "Your house is beautiful. Did you buy one of those log cabin kits?"

"Not at all. I bought logs and did all the work myself. It took me three years between jobs and on the weekends, but I love this place. I have three bedrooms and two baths. I would say my kitchen has all the modern conveniences, but compared to the one I put in at your house, it has nothing."

Alyssa laughed softly. "Well, we did go just a bit overboard on that kitchen."

Nick opened the door and watched her face as she stepped inside. She stood—holding the grocery bags—in the middle of his living room and spun in a small circle. "I love this! It feels so homey." She put the bags onto the counter and wandered around opening doors.

There was a spare bedroom with a king bed made up in it. "My parents stay there when they visit," he said.

"Very cozy." There was a quilt on the bed that had obviously been lovingly pieced. "I like this quilt."

"My grandmother made it. Mom said if she can't be at home, she wants to feel like she is." Nick waited until she was finished in there. He opened the next door for her. "This is going to eventually be a bedroom, but for now I store stuff in here. I need to build a shed, but there hasn't been time."

She nodded, walking into the room and looking at the closet. "I love these big walk-in closets. They're so perfect." She opened another door and saw that it was a bathroom, connecting the two bedrooms. "I'm sure this is convenient for guests as well."

He nodded. "It is. I love it." Together they walked to the last door leading off of the main rooms. "Now, this room isn't quite as neat." He opened the door, and she peeked in at his bedroom.

It showed his personality, she thought. "I like it, though." There were wrinkles in the bed that had been hurriedly made. There was an overflowing hamper in the corner of the room. "We haven't been giving you any time to do laundry!" Why hadn't she thought of that before?

He shrugged. "I don't like laundry anyway."

She laughed. "Well, I don't mind if you do it while I'm here."

"But . . . what if you see my tighty whities?"

Alyssa shook her head at him. "I guess I'd melt into a puddle of wanton passion if I saw such a thing."

"Then I'm definitely doing my laundry while you're here." Nick winked at her.

Poking her head into the bathroom, she saw a huge bathtub and a shower. "I like this!" She turned to him and grinned. "You did a good job!"

"Thank you. I designed it as well as building it. I should probably have Amanda come in and decorate it, but I like it as it is."

"I do, too." She walked out of the bedroom and back into the main area of the home, looking around a little more. It had an open concept, and the living room, dining area, and kitchen were all basically one big room. "So, I don't need to start cooking for a few hours. Why don't we put the groceries away, and we can watch a movie?"

He nodded. "I'd love that. And I'm putting a load of laundry in the washer, too."

"I didn't see a washer dryer." She looked around her, trying to figure out where it was hidden.

"That's because I didn't show you the basement. It's down there, and I don't expect you to follow me down."

She shrugged. "Then you start the load, and I'll put the groceries away. We'll meet on the couch when we're done."

"Sounds good to me."

"You need a laundry chute!" she told him as he walked away.

He laughed. "I have one. I just haven't been down there in a while, and the pile got so high, I couldn't put anything else through it."

"Wow. Okay. It really is time we gave you a day off."

TWENTY-SIX

On Monday while Alyssa went to Salt Lake City, Nick went shopping with Amanda instead of working on the house. He'd discussed the possibility of the shopping trip with the sisters while Alyssa had been taking her real estate exam. He needed help picking out the perfect engagement ring, and he knew Amanda would know Alyssa's taste better than anyone.

When they returned, the other sisters demanded to see the ring. He felt strange with all of them knowing he was about to propose, but he didn't know what else to do, so he pulled the ring out of his pocket and opened the box.

Lauren put her hand over her heart. "You're making me swoon, Nick. If Alyssa says 'no,' all you have to do is ask me."

He chuckled, a bit embarrassed by all the attention.

Taylor simply looked at the ring and nodded. "That's perfect. You two did good."

He tucked the ring back into his pocket and got back to work, determined to make up for the half day lost while he'd been ring shopping in Logan.

As he worked, he whistled, happier than he could ever remember being. Alyssa was the love of his life, and though he hadn't known her long, he didn't need to. She was perfect, and he was going to ask her very soon.

Alyssa talked to her sisters when she got back from Salt Lake City the next day. "Kayla said to hug everyone for her."

"I'm so glad you decided to stay with her rather than going to a hotel. She needed some sister time," Lauren said. "Every time we've talked lately, she's seemed more and more bummed that she's not here with us. I really feel badly for her."

Amanda nodded. "She's got to feel all alone."

"She seems to," Alyssa said. "I'm really glad I spent the time with her." She walked into the living room, and all of her sisters followed her. "There's something I've been wanting to talk to you guys about."

"What's that?" Taylor asked, sitting beside her. "Is something wrong?"

"No, not wrong. I just . . . well, I think we need to start giving Nick a day off every week. He's working so hard, and I just think he needs a day every week for laundry and grocery shopping. He did six loads of laundry Friday while I was there. I'm sure he didn't have many clothes left."

Amanda bit her lip. "I think you're right. We really are overworking the poor man."

"Kayla thinks she can be here by June first. We have two bedrooms ready for Amanda to work her magic, and we'll have a few more by then. When they both start working, they can knock the others out quickly," Lauren said. "I think it's a good idea."

Taylor nodded. "You're right. I just want everything to be done before the first, but we have to think about how we're half-killing him."

"Yes, we do," Alyssa said, glad the others had all agreed with her. "And I think we could use a day without a man in the house."

Amanda laughed. "A day without Nick? What will you ever do?"

"Hopefully he'll take advantage of the time off to spend with his girl," Alyssa said, winking at the others.

There was general laughter.

"Fine. We'll tell him in the morning." Lauren got to her feet. "Are you hungry? I made beef tips to serve over rice, and there's some left in the crock pot."

"That sounds fabulous. I haven't eaten since noon." It was well after seven. Alyssa hadn't been thinking clearly and had left Salt Lake City at four, hitting rush hour. It was nice not to think much about rush hour anymore.

"Come on," Lauren said. "I'll feed you."

JUST AS SHE'D HOPED, Nick had asked Alyssa to spend Sunday afternoon with him. He was supposed to pick her up around two, and she was ready and waiting when the doorbell rang. She had no idea what he had in mind, so she'd dressed in jeans and a t-shirt with a hoodie over it. He wasn't a formal kind of guy, so that should work out just fine.

She ran to the door, excited to see him. It had been almost twenty hours since she'd last touched him, and that was *way* too long. Touching him was like a slice of chocolate cake after a twenty-four–hour fast.

She threw the door open with a huge smile on her face. "Hey . . ." Her smile faded and her eyes grew wide. "What are *you* doing here?"

Tim was on her doorstep, and he had one of his smirks on his face. The kind of half-smile she'd once thought was so adorable but now made her feel a bit sick to her stomach. "I missed you."

She narrowed her eyes. "How did you find me?" She certainly hadn't given him a forwarding address, and she knew none of the people in her life would have told him.

"It's not like you were hiding from me." He shrugged. "I realize I've made some mistakes with you, and I want to apologize."

"I see." Alyssa really didn't want to forgive the man, but she knew deep down inside that forgiving him would be good for her. Hanging on to her anger wouldn't help anything at all. "I forgive you. Thanks for coming to see me." She started to close the door, but he once again shoved his foot in it. "Is there something else?"

Tim nodded, dropping to one knee there on her doorstep. Alyssa wanted to throw up. There was no way he was proposing now. It was all she'd wanted for years and years, and now it was the last thing in the world she'd ever want. "Alyssa, will you marry me?"

TWENTY-SEVEN

Nick put on a button-up shirt and tie for the first time in forever. He was sure the last time he'd worn one had been to his grandmother's funeral. It was strange that you wore the same things for the happy times as well as the sad. He looked in the mirror and combed his hair, wanting to look his best for Alyssa.

He walked out to his truck and realized his hand was shaking a little. He knew it was probably going to feel strange to her that he was proposing so soon, but he knew she was the one he wanted to spend the rest of his life with, so he wasn't sure why he should wait.

He drove to her house but parked around the corner, wanting to surprise her with a walk on the beach, where he would take her hands in his and beg her to spend the rest of her life with him.

As he walked, he mentally practiced what he was going to say, wanting everything to be perfect. Thankfully it wasn't snowing for a change, and a walk on the beach wouldn't seem strange to her.

He walked to the front door, instead of the back door as he had since he'd started working there and stopped on the sidewalk facing the house.

Alyssa was in the doorway with one hand over her mouth, and a man he'd never seen before was on one knee on the doorstep. Nick turned and walked away, feeling as if a knife had just been stabbed through his heart. Whoever the man was, she hadn't seemed to be turning him down. No, with her hand over her mouth that way, she was obviously happy. It was how he'd imagined she'd look when he held out the ring and asked her to marry him.

He ran back to the car, thankful he'd worn jeans and tennis shoes with his dress shirt. Yes, it was strange, but now he was glad.

He got in his truck and drove, wondering why seeing her that way had hurt so much more than seeing Kami in bed with another man. Both women had betrayed him, but one was so much worse than the other.

He turned his car toward Logan Canyon, wanting to drive the difficult roads so he could stop thinking about seeing her that way. This way the drive would be a challenge and he would have to concentrate. Anything to not think about his hopes and dreams being washed away like footprints in the sand.

Alyssa stared at Tim in shock for a moment. "No, I will *not* marry you." She said nothing else as she closed the door. She ran up the stairs, hoping to find at least one of her sisters. There was no way she was going to be able to go out with Nick right away. She had to shower first and wash away how dirty his proposal had made her feel.

She swallowed hard, hoping to keep herself from vomiting. That wasn't what she'd wanted or expected. Not in any way.

She went to Taylor's room and found her sister sitting at her desk, busily writing on some paper in front of her. "Would you be willing to go downstairs and wait for Nick? I need to shower. Badly."

Taylor heard something wrong with her sister's voice and turned to her. "What happened?" She got to her feet. "Your face is pure white."

"Tim. He came by and asked me to forgive him. I knew that

forgiving him would keep me from being angry, so I said I would, and then I tried to close the door, but he stuck his foot in it. Again."

"Okay. He didn't hurt you, did he?" Taylor was looking more concerned by the moment.

Alyssa took a ragged breath. "He got down on one knee and asked me to marry him. So, I told him no and slammed the door in his face. For all I know, he's still out there, waiting for me to 'come to my senses.'" Alyssa used air quotes when she talked about coming to her senses.

Taylor shook her head, looking angry. "I'll go down and see if he's still there. I'd love it if he was still on his knees so I could easily kick him in the face."

Alyssa couldn't help but smile at that. "I love you, Taylor."

"I love you, too!" Taylor hurried toward the stairs while Alyssa got into the shower, wanting to scrub every inch of her body. How on earth had she ever thought she loved that man? He wasn't worth her time. He wasn't even worth her being upset. She was going to spend the day with Nick, a man who knew how to give and receive love. He was the only man she ever wanted to be with for the rest of her life.

She'd been hoping he would ask her to marry him, and instead, she'd gotten Tim. She wanted to throw up again, but she put her hand on her stomach for a moment before soaping up everywhere. She had to be able to wash off the feeling she had. There was nothing else to do.

When she got downstairs, it was thirty minutes after Nick was supposed to be there for their date. She didn't ask Taylor if Tim had still been there when she got downstairs, because she truly didn't want to know. She never even wanted to hear the man's name again, let alone think of him asking her to marry him. Or hanging around Bear Lake. She'd never been with him in that house, and it had made it feel safe. Now the house even felt wrong.

She sat on the couch, looking over at Taylor. "Did Nick come?"

Taylor shook her head. "I haven't seen or heard from him. I hope he wasn't in a wreck."

The idea scared Alyssa. "I'm going to drive over to his place and make sure of that. I can't imagine him missing a date unless there was an emergency. I hope he's all right."

Taylor nodded. "Go. I'll let him know that's where you went if he comes by."

Alyssa hurried out to her vehicle and drove to Nick's cabin, pushing the speed limit a little more than she usually would. His truck wasn't in the driveway, and she knew that's where he usually parked it. So, where was he?

She picked up her phone and dialed his number, but it went straight to voicemail. She said a silent prayer for his safety and drove back toward the house. Wherever he was, she just needed for him to be unhurt. She couldn't imagine living even a day without seeing him anymore.

When she got home, all three of her sisters were in the living room. Obviously, Taylor had filled the other two in.

"Have you heard anything?" Alyssa asked.

Taylor shook her head. "Not a word. I even tried to call him, but there was no answer."

"I did, too. It went straight to voicemail." Alyssa frowned. "I'm going to go upstairs and keep trying."

Lauren put her hand on Alyssa's arm. "I know it's been a hard day, but we're all here for you. Anything you need, you just tell us."

Alyssa felt a single tear escape her eye. "I just need to know he's okay."

"I'll call the hospital," Amanda said. "If he's hurt, they'll know."

"Good idea. Thank you!" Alyssa hurried toward the stairs, needing to be alone as she called him. Over and over for the rest of the day, she dialed his number and listened as it went to voicemail.

Finally, she threw herself on her bed and cried. First Tim had shown up where he didn't belong and was unwelcome. And then Nick had disappeared. It was too much for her to handle.

TWENTY-EIGHT

Nick thought long and hard about whether he wanted to go back to the Romriell house and continue working there after what had happened. He was up half the night thinking about it, and finally decided that he needed to. He had made a commitment, and he wasn't about to leave a job half done. He also didn't want Alyssa to think she'd hurt him, even though she really had.

Getting ready for work the following morning, he was both annoyed and nervous. He wasn't sure how he was going to be able to look at Alyssa without being hurt and angry, but he was going to have to try. Hopefully she'd be going to her office and getting it ready to actually start working there. That would be the best-case scenario for him.

He walked in the back door of the house shortly before seven and went to the next room he needed to start working on. Thankfully it was a downstairs bedroom, and there would be little chance of running into Alyssa there. He had a list of the things that needed to be changed, and the colors the room needed to be painted. He would focus on the task at hand and pretend no women even lived in the house.`

He was only fifteen minutes into his day when Alyssa appeared at the door of the room he was working in.

"Are you okay?" she asked, her face concerned.

He barely glanced at her before continuing with the task at hand. "Sure."

"You didn't come yesterday. We were supposed to meet at two."

"I got busy," he lied. He had no desire to talk to her ever again. Why didn't she just go away?

"You didn't call, and I left you fifteen voicemails."

"Don't you think that's a little excessive?" he asked, staring straight ahead. "If I didn't show up, wouldn't it have made sense that I had no desire to see you?"

He heard her slight intake of breath, and she sounded hurt to him. He didn't want to hurt her, but he was so hurt himself, he didn't know how else to get rid of her.

"I don't know what I did to make you angry," Alyssa said, her voice sounding like she was on the verge of tears.

He straightened his spine and looked at her. "Then I guess you'll never know." He moved to another wall with his paint roller, his back to her now. "Go away, Alyssa. Go and set up your new office or go back to Salt Lake where you belong." She had to belong in Salt Lake City. Where else would that man have come from?

He heard her footsteps walking away from him, and he had to stifle the urge to call her back and beg her forgiveness for the way he'd just spoken to her. She was acting like the injured party, when they both knew that wasn't true at all.

Nick closed his eyes for a moment, taking a deep breath to center himself. He had to get through this job and onto the next one. He couldn't let this derail him completely.

Alyssa went to her room, changed into a pair of leggings and a t-shirt, and put her running shoes on. All she wanted to do was cry, but first she needed to run. Running would help her deal with her emotions.

Instead of going to the beach, where her memories of Nick would plague her, she ran through the streets, heading for a country road. She had left her phone at the house on purpose, not wanting anyone to bother her as she ran off the emotions.

She ran toward Fish Haven, simply wanting to be out of town, where people were starting to think of her and Nick as an item. In Salt Lake City when she'd broken up with Tim, she hadn't really run into anyone who asked her about it. Here, she knew things would be different. Small town life was wonderful most of the time, but in this case, she wasn't terribly excited about it.

She ran and ran, finally glancing down at her watch and seeing she'd already gone five miles. It was time to turn around and go home, and she prayed she'd make it. Hopefully her aching muscles would give her something to focus on other than Nick.

By the time she got back to the house, she had tears streaming down her face. She went straight to her room and the shower, not wanting to talk or look at anyone. Maybe she needed to move out faster than planned so her sisters wouldn't ask her about Nick. She couldn't even face them at the moment. They'd all thought he was a good one, unlike Tim. Why was she incapable of realizing a man would break her heart into a million pieces until it was in the process of happening?

She changed into her oldest, rattiest pair of pajamas and laid on her bed, curling into a ball and sobbing. Ending a one-month relationship had become so much harder than ending a seven-year partnership. How could that be?

There was a knock on her door, and she called, "Go away!" her voice as ragged as her pajamas.

Amanda opened the door and stood there for a moment, looking at her with concern. She stepped inside and closed the door behind her. Walking over to the bed, she sat down beside her sister, and stroked her hair away from her face. "What happened?"

Alyssa cried even harder, unable to find her voice for a moment. When she did finally talk, her speech was broken up and involved a great deal of struggling for breath. "Nick . . . dumped me. And he . . . won't even . . . tell me why."

"What? No way! Nick loves you, Alyssa. I don't know what just happened, but that man is head over heels for you, and you need to work this out."

"He . . . won't talk . . . to me."

Amanda frowned. "Wait until he goes home from work tonight and go to his house. Walk in without knocking, and corner him. Don't let him make you leave until he's told you what's really going on. He promised us he would never hurt you, and you need to get to the bottom of this. I know something had to have happened."

Alyssa didn't respond. She couldn't. She had no breath to speak.

"Wait . . . is it possible he came by while Tim was here yesterday? Could he have seen him . . . be an idiot?"

Looking up at her sister, Alyssa brushed the tears from her eyes. "Maybe?"

"I bet that's what happened. Have you ever told Nick about Tim?"

Alyssa shook her head. "Not really."

Groaning softly, Amanda got to her feet. "I'm going to go get you a bottle of water, and you're going to go see him tonight. First, though, we sisters are going to go out to lunch, and you're going to figure out how to stop crying. While I'm gone, get those pajamas off and get dressed. No wallowing. This will be all fixed soon."

Following her sister's orders, Alyssa got up and changed into real clothes, but she wasn't as convinced as Amanda was that anything could be fixed. How could it be better when Nick hated her now?

Fresh tears started again, and she went into the bathroom to wash her face with a cold cloth. They couldn't eat in town because too many people there knew her now. No, they'd have to drive to Logan and eat somewhere there. She was craving Olive Garden, and her sisters could just go and watch her eat if they didn't want it. She needed to be pampered for a change.

Maybe there was a place in Logan to get a pedicure, too. That would make her feel a little better and give her the courage to face Nick. Something had to.

TWENTY-NINE

AFTER SPENDING the day in Logan with her sisters, Alyssa got in her car and headed to Nick's house. It was after eight, so she knew he'd be home, and hopefully he would be receptive to everything she had to say. She wasn't going to back down, though. She never would have fought for Tim, but fighting for Nick was a no-brainer.

She pulled into his driveway and parked right behind his truck, walking to his house, taking a deep breath, and opening the door. She walked in and marched straight to his couch, where he was sitting.

He looked at her with a shocked expression on his face. "I didn't invite you."

"No, you didn't, but you're going to listen to me, Nick Peot, because I think our relationship is worth it." She took a deep breath. "I haven't really talked to you about Tim, a man I dated in Salt Lake City. I wasn't trying to hide it from you, but I wasn't proud of what happened between us, and I'm going to tell you all about it now." She sat down on the couch beside him, curling one leg under her and facing him. "Tim and I started dating seven years ago. We met when he went house shopping with a client of mine."

Nick turned to her. "I'm not sure what this has to do with us."

"It has a *lot* to do with us. Please listen to everything I have to say, and then if you still want me to leave, I will." Alyssa couldn't force him to accept what she said and love her back. But he would know how she felt before she left his home.

He nodded, looking surprised. "All right."

"Thank you. Anyway, Tim and I started dating, and at first, he would tell me how beautiful I was and act like he cared for me a great deal." She took a breath, finding telling him about this was more difficult than she'd thought it would be. "So, after a few months, he told me I was getting pudgy and he wanted me to work out with a friend of his. He started telling me I had to lose weight and commenting on it all the time. I was already slender, but I lost more than twelve pounds working with his trainer and cutting out sugar." She shrugged. "Well, except for my Junior Mint addiction." She pulled a box out of the pocket of her hoodie and showed it to him, popping one of them into her mouth. She offered him the box, but he shook his head.

"You know you're perfect, right?" Nick asked her.

Alyssa shrugged. "I know now he was playing mind games with me." Sighing dramatically, she continued, "He would tell me my hair was too long, and then it was too short. I needed to dye it a different color, because he didn't want to be seen with a 'mouse.' He slowly chipped away at my self-esteem, asking me to change everything about the way I looked. Within a year of us starting dating, he lost his job, and he came to me for a 'loan.' While he was floundering at work, I was kicking major butt. I was earning all kinds of awards for being the top salesperson in my region. So, I loaned him the money. That was the first of many loans, and he never paid me back a dime."

"Sounds like he really did a number on you."

"He did. Shortly before my parents died, he started spending less and less time with me. He had things to do with his guy friends, and he was too busy for me, even though he was once again unemployed. For me, the catalyst came right after two policemen came and told me about my parents' death. I called him before I even called my sisters, needing someone to talk to who didn't know them well and could comfort me without me having to comfort them as well. He was at a party, and he made it very clear that he thought I was stupid for calling him and I needed to hang up and call my sisters." Alyssa shook her head, remembering how she'd felt at that moment. "Until then, I thought we were just going through a rough patch but that we were still deeply in love."

"He sounds like someone I'd like to put my fist through." Nick shook his head. "I have a hard time seeing you let yourself be a victim that way."

"I've gotten stronger. My sisters have been my rocks—as well as Hannah, of course. I don't know what I would have done without the five of them." She stood up, pacing a little, because now she was getting close to the difficult part of the discussion. "So, after the lawyer read the will to us, Taylor suggested the B&B. I knew I needed a change after everything that had happened, so I agreed. I started to say I couldn't leave because of Tim, but my sisters weren't having any of that. They were all worried I was anorexic, and I know I was probably close. If it weren't for the Junior Mints . . ."

He grinned at that, and his lopsided smile sent a bolt of lightning to her heart. If he could stop looking at her as if she'd killed the feelings he had for her, then maybe they could make this work.

"He came to the door a few minutes later, and I told him I was done with him. He kept trying to talk me out of it, but for once, I was able to stay strong. He finally asked if we could be friends, and I told him no. There was too much water under the bridge for that. Then he asked for another 'loan,' and Taylor came over and slammed the door on his foot."

Nick laughed softly. "Good for Taylor!"

"Yeah. Good for Taylor. Anyway, he came back a few weeks later, asking me to reconsider. Lauren was with me, and when he wouldn't take no for an answer, she made sure he saw reason. We moved a few days later, and I was sure I'd seen the last of him. It wasn't like I'd told him my plans or given him a forwarding address."

She moved back to sit beside him, wishing she dared to reach out and touch him, but she was afraid of what his reaction would be. "Then the doorbell rang on Sunday, about when you were supposed to get there, and I thought you'd be on the other side of the door when I opened it. I was so happy and excited to see you and spend some time together. But it wasn't you. It was Tim."

He put his hand over hers, and she knew it was all going to be all right. He didn't hate her anymore.

"So, anyway, he asked me to forgive him, and I said I would, knowing that forgiving him was something I needed to do for me so I could let go of the anger I'd been feeling for so long."

"Sure."

Alyssa sighed. "When I said I'd forgive him, he immediately took my hand and went down on one knee on my doorstep and asked me to marry him. I'd waited *seven years* for him to ask me that, but after I'd fallen in love with you, there he was." She shook her head. "The man is a boil on the butt of humanity, and I have no desire to ever look at him again."

"And then I walked up, saw the shocked—and I thought pleased—look on your face, and I assumed you were happy he was proposing. I thought you'd say yes and marry him. So, I turned and left."

"Yeah, Amanda and I put that together after I talked to you this morning. After I shut the door on him, I went upstairs and took a shower, wanting to wash with bleach and a Brillo Pad." She turned her hand over and grasped his with hers. "I left Taylor to deal with Tim, if he was still there. I have no idea what happened, because I slammed the door in his face. She was supposed to watch for you. I probably took a half-hour shower just to get his touch off my skin. When I went back downstairs, she said you hadn't been by, which bothered me a little, but I figured you were just running late. And then I called you, and it went straight to voicemail. I spent the rest of the day worried you'd been killed in a car accident or something else terrible had happened to you. It never occurred to me that you could have seen Tim."

"I did, though. I should have talked to you instead of just reacting." Nick frowned. "I wish I had."

"Me too. But I understand you getting upset, because I hadn't really told you about him, and I should have. Much sooner than I did."

He leaned forward and pressed his forehead to hers. "Do you know why it hurt that much?"

She shook her head. "No, not really."

He got up and walked to the fireplace, taking a small box off the mantle. "Because I was going to invite you for a walk on the beach and see if you wanted to wear this engagement ring." He opened the box and held it out to her.

She gasped as she stared at it, a hand going over her mouth, just as he'd imagined it would. "I . . ."

"I know we haven't known one another long, and I know we don't know everything about each other yet, but I love you with everything inside me. I know that you're the woman I'm meant to spend my life with. I'm sorry I botched everything up so badly."

"You didn't. Tim did." She stared at the ring, which was a diamond surrounded by tiny sapphires—her birthstone. "Am I going to get another chance at that ring?"

He grinned, sitting beside her and taking both of her hands in his. "You have another chance at it now. Alyssa Romriell, will you add my initial to your monogram?" It wasn't what he'd rehearsed and planned to say, but it fit. It's what he wanted more than anything else on earth.

"Yes. A million times yes!" She threw her arms around him and clung to him for dear life. "You're everything I want."

"Well, I kind of want kids, too . . ."

"We need to have five little girls who can learn to laugh and love at the lake."

"I'm not sure about five . . ." He used his index finger and tilted her face to meet his. His lips slowly descended, and he kissed her softly. "So . . . when? I want to be married yesterday."

She grinned at him, her hand going to his cheek and caressing it. "I can't make it happen yesterday, but why don't we do it in mid-June? Our first wedding at the B&B."

He nodded. "I would love that. I guess I'll need to work on a gazebo there."

"Yes, you will!" Alyssa laughed softly, happier than she'd ever dreamed she'd be. But maybe that was why dreams changed, so she could grow into a happier person.

"You plan the wedding, and I'll build the gazebo."

"That's a deal." She pulled him to her for another kiss, finally feeling like her life was going in the right direction.

EPILOGUE

Taylor stood on the edge of the lake, looking out over the clear, blue waters. She was glad Alyssa and Nick had worked things out, but that's not what she wanted for herself. She couldn't see herself as someone's wife, having two point three children or whatever the national average was these days. No, she was going to continue working on Romriell House and turn it into the best darn B&B the area had ever seen.

She turned to walk up the path that led back to the house. They only had a week until the first guests started arriving. She could see where Nick had blocked out a spot for the gazebo he and Alyssa planned to marry in, and she smiled.

Her dreams were coming true.

ABOUT THE AUTHOR

KIRSTEN OSBOURNE hails from the state of Wisconsin, but has lived in Texas for almost thirty years. She is a mother, a writer, and a wife. Married to the love of her life for over fifteen years, she knows that true love exists and wants to share her vision of love with the world. Writing is something she has always loved and plans on doing for a long time into the future. Kirsten Osbourne writes contemporary romance as well as historical. She invites you to join her in her world of fantasy and make believe where there is always a happily ever after at the end.

www.kirstenaOsbourne.com

ALSO BY KIRSTEN OSBOURNE

Sign up for instant notification of all of Kirsten's New Releases Text 'BOB' to 42828

And

For a complete list of Kirsten's works head to her website wwww.kirstenosbourne.com

CPSIA information can be obtained
at www.ICGtesting.com
Printed in the USA
LVHW041454120819
627342LV00007B/988

9 781937 915957